12-17

The Hoosier School-Master

The Hoosier

School-Master

A NOVEL BY EDWARD EGGLESTON

INTRODUCTION BY VERNON LOGGINS
Professor Emeritus of English, Columbia University

AMERICAN CENTURY SERIES

HILL AND WANG · NEW YORK

FIRST AMERICAN CENTURY SERIES EDITION APRIL 1957

11 12 13 14

INTRODUCTION

The *Hoosier School-Master* was published, both as magazine serial and as independent volume, in 1871. The book immediately met with popular favor. The hundreds of thousands who read it thought of it as a novel which, like *Little Women* and *Tom Sawyer,* offered excellent entertainment to adults as well as to children. Early in the twentieth century critics began to single it out as an accurate picture of a vanishing phase of American civilization. Today it is offered in schools and colleges as a landmark in American literature—an effectual force in the development of realistic fiction in America and a monument in American regional writing.

Edward Eggleston himself, when he hastily wrote *The Hoosier School-Master* at the age of thirty-four, could not have dreamed that he was creating a literary landmark. He simply brought into service his fine memory, and wrote with the over-all aim of reaching the hearts of his readers.

He had passed the most impressionable years of his life, the first thirteen, either in his birthplace—Vevay, Switzerland County, Indiana—or on his maternal grandfather's farm, several miles to the north. Though Vevay had a population of only about a thousand, it was an Ohio River port and served the entire southeastern corner of Indiana as a trading center. Of the numerous cultivated families in the town, not one was more highly respected than the Egglestons. The father, who had grown up on a plantation in Amelia County, Virginia, had been counted among the most brilliant students ever graduated from the College of William and Mary. He was a leading lawyer in Vevay and a prominent figure in politics. The mother was the daughter of Captain George Craig, famed in Indiana for his youthful exploits as frontiersman and Indian fighter. The Eggleston children were in the habit of spending weeks on stretch at Captain Craig's farm. The death of their father, in 1846, meant little change in the pattern of their lives. But when, on Christmas Day, 1850, their mother married a Methodist minister, the Eggleston home was definitely broken up.

The eldest son, Edward, then thirteen, and the second son, George Cary, eleven, had been manifesting all their lives an astounding precocity. Their father, seeing that such schools as were available would do them more harm than good, had taught them at home as long as he lived. After his death their mother, stressing the tenets of Methodism, which forbid even the handling of a novel, had taken over their instruction. But the two boys had had other teachers of inestimable value—the backwoods Hoosiers with whom they had mingled on their grandfather's farm and on the streets and wharves of Vevay on market days.

For the next six years Edward and George, more often separated than in one another's company, drifted from place to place. Edward spent several months on an uncle's farm in Decatur County, Indiana, where he encountered a Hoosier primitiveness even more rugged than in Switzerland County; he stayed for long periods with his mother when she was living in New Albany, across the Ohio River from Louisville, and again when she was living in Madison, up the Ohio, nearer Switzerland County; he returned to Vevay for a term at the town academy, where a teacher urged him to cultivate his talent for writing; and he passed a year and a half on the Eggleston ancestral plantation in Virginia, attending the academy at Amelia Courthouse.

Towards the end of his stay in Virginia a relative offered to send him to the University in Charlottesville. He refused, saying that he did not wish to go to a college supported by a state which legalized slavery. Perhaps his unpolitic reply explains why George and not he, the elder, fell heir to the Eggleston plantation in 1856.

In the late summer of that year George, no doubt in fine clothes and possibly with a Negro slave to attend him, entered the College of Richmond as a student of law. At the same time Edward, who believed that God had called him to preach the Gospel according to the Methodist creed, somehow got possession of horse, saddle, and saddle bags, and, a self-appointed preacher, began his career as a circuit rider. Although he had taught himself Latin, Greek, higher mathematics, and all the other branches of learning then required for a college degree, he had not studied theology. His opinion was that with a volume of John Wesley's sermons, Charles Wesley's hymns, and a Bible in one of his saddle bags he had at hand all the theology needed.

His circuit, deep in the country north of Vevay, was made up of ten "preaching places," at each of which he appeared at least once a month. At last he was an intimate of the Hoosier backwoodsmen who had fascinated him all of his life. He rode with them over the rough trails and muddy roads, he slept in their cabins, he ate at their tables, he united them in marriage, he christened their babies, he went with them on 'coon hunts, he took part in their spelling matches, he spoke with them in their idiom, and many a time he had their bodies quaking in terror or rolling on the floor after he had preached a sermon on the plight of the damned on the day of doom. All the time he passed in their presence he was observing them with a discernment they would have called miraculous if they could have known of it.

But a single winter of the hardships of riding circuit was all the frail body of the nineteen-year-old youth could stand. Convinced that he had consumption and was in the shadow of death, he left in April, 1857, for the pine country of Minnesota.

Within his psyche the groundwork for the creation of *The Hoosier School-Master* had been laid. His activities during the next fourteen years—holding small Methodist pastorates in Minnesota, getting married, regaining his health, selling stories and sketches to juvenile and religious magazines, editing such periodicals in Chicago and New York, moving in the direction of an individualistic liberalism in his religious thinking, reading fiction at last and admiring Dickens—really did little to strengthen him for the supreme achievement of his life.

His reunion with his brother in 1870 spurred him to this act. George, after fighting in the Confederate army throughout the war, had returned to Amelia County only to sell the Eggleston plantation in order to satisfy the demands of his creditors. He then had lost his last cent in a banking venture in southern Illinois, and had failed in an attempt to practice law in the state of Mississippi. In the fall of 1870 he turned up in New York with his wife and one child, and through Edward's help found employment as reporter for the Brooklyn *Daily Eagle*. In the summer of 1871, when Edward was on the staff of the *Independent*, he and George were given the opportunity to work as colleagues in editing *Hearth and Home*. They accepted the offer.

In doing so they knew that they were exchanging security for uncertainty. For *Hearth and Home* was in grave financial difficulties. If it survived, it had to be given new life. While George, who bore himself with the dignity and elegance of General Lee, went out to find new writers, Edward, who with his long hair and rich beard still looked the part of the Methodist minister, stayed in his office trying to summon from the inner reaches of his mind the idea for a serial which would stir the readers of *Hearth and Home*.

In the summer of 1871 all America was reading or discussing Bret Harte and his volume, then just a year old, *The Luck of Roaring Camp and Other Sketches*. If the Americans were so interested in the imagined doings of the roughs who flocked to California in the 1850's to dig for gold, wouldn't they also be interested in the actual doings of the backwoodsmen of Indiana?

George suggested a plot, his own experiences in teaching school in upper Switzerland County when he was only sixteen. Edward's inner sense accepted this idea as good, and *The Hoosier School-Master* was begun.

Edward got the first installment ready for the September 30 issue of *Hearth and Home*. Then day after day, at hours when he was free of editorial duties, he wrote, following a simple line of action such as he had found in the juveniles of the time, presenting the characters as cartoons rather than as portraits, throwing in an abundance of Hoosier humor, giving enough sentimentality to please the teary-eyed, striving for photographic truth in every picture, echoing Dickens occasionally and the Bible often, and expressing himself always in the short sentences which were to become fashionable long after his death. By December 30, when the last installment appeared, the volume was on the shelves of bookstores throughout America.

So was born *The Hoosier School-Master*, which is to Americans what Mrs. Gaskell's *Cranford* is to the English and what Daudet's *Lettres de mon Moulin* is to the French —a book all compact of that inexplicable something called charm.

VERNON LOGGINS

Columbia University

CONTENTS

PREFACE

I may as well confess, what it would be affectation to conceal, that I am more than pleased with the generous reception accorded to this story as a serial in the columns of *Hearth and Home*. It has been in my mind since I was a Hoosier boy to do something toward describing life in the back-country districts of the Western States. It used to be a matter of no little jealousy with us, I remember, that the manners, customs, thoughts, and feelings of New England country people filled so large a place in books, while our life, not less interesting, not less romantic, and certainly not less filled with humorous and grotesque material, had no place in literature. It was as though we were shut out of good society. And, with the single exception of Alice Cary, perhaps, our Western writers did not dare speak of the West otherwise than as the unreal world to which Cooper's lively imagination had given birth.

I had some anxiety lest Western readers should take offense at my selecting what must always seem an exceptional phase of life to those who have grown up in the more refined regions of the West. But nowhere has the School-master been received more kindly than in his own country and among his own people.

Some of those who have spoken kindly of the School-master and his friends, have suggested that the story is an autobiography. But it is not, save in the sense in which every work of art is an autobiography, in that it is the result of the experience and observation of the writer. Readers will therefore bear in mind that not Ralph nor Bud nor Brother Sodom nor Dr. Small represents the writer, nor do I appear, as Talleyrand said of Madame de Stael, "disguised as a woman," in the person of Hannah or Mirandy. Some of the incidents have been drawn from life; none of them, I believe, from my own. I should like to be considered a member of the Church of the Best Licks, however.

It has been in my mind to append some remarks, philological and otherwise, upon the dialect, but Professor Lowell's admirable and erudite preface to the Biglow Papers must be the despair of every one who aspires to write on Americanisms. To Mr. Lowell belongs the distinction of being the only one of our most eminent authors and the only one of our most eminent scholars who has given careful attention to American dialects. But while I have not ventured to discuss the provincialisms of the Indiana backwoods, I have been careful to preserve the true *usus loquendi* of each locution, and I trust my little story may afford material for some one better qualified than I to criticise the dialect.

I wish to dedicate this book to Rev. Williamson Terrell, D.D., of Columbus, Indiana, the Hoosier that I know best, and the best Hoosier that I know. This is not the place to express the reverence and filial affection I feel for him, but I am glad of the opportunity of saying that there is no one to whom Southern Indiana owes a larger debt. Perhaps my dedication to so orthodox a man may atone for any heresies in the book.

Brooklyn, December, 1871

xiv

I

A Private Lesson from a Bull-Dog

"Want to be a school-master, do you? You? Well, what would *you* do in Flat Crick deestrick, *I'd* like to know? Why, the boys have driv off the last two, and licked the one afore them like blazes. You might teach a summer school, when nothin' but children come. But I 'low it takes a right smart *man* to be school-master in Flat Crick in the winter. They'd pitch you out of doors, sonny, neck and heels, afore Christmas."

The young man, who had walked ten miles to get the school in this district, and who had been mentally reviewing his learning at every step he took, trembling lest the committee should find that he did not know enough, was not a little taken aback at this greeting from "old Jack Means," who was the first trustee that he lighted on. The impression made by these ominous remarks was emphasized by the glances which he received from Jack 'Means' two sons. The older one eyed him from the top of his brawny shoulders with that amiable look which a big dog turns on a little one before shaking him. Ralph Hartsook had never thought of being measured by the standard of muscle. This notion of beating education into

1

young savages in spite of themselves, dashed his ardor.

He had walked right to where Jack Means was at work shaving shingles in his own front yard. While Mr. Means was making the speech which we have set down above, and punctuating it with expectorations, a large brindle bull-dog had been sniffing at Ralph's heels, and a girl in a new linsey-woolsey dress, standing by the door, had nearly giggled her head off at the delightful prospect of seeing a new school-teacher eaten up by the ferocious brute.

Between the disheartening words of the old man, the immense muscles of the young man who was to be his rebellious pupil, the jaws of the ugly bull-dog, and the heartless giggle of the girl, Ralph had a delightful sense of having precipitated himself into a den of wild beasts. Faint with weariness and discouragement, and shivering with fear, he sat down on a wheelbarrow.

"You, Bull!" said the old man to the dog, which was showing more and more a disposition to make a meal of the incipient pedagogue, "you, Bull! git aout, you pup!" The dog walked sullenly off, but not until he had given Ralph a look full of promise of what he meant to do when he got a good chance. Ralph wished himself back in the village of Lewisburg, whence he had come.

"You see," continued Mr. Means, spitting in a meditative sort of a way, "you see, we a'n't none of your saft sort in these diggins. It takes a *man* to boss this deestrick. Howsumdever, ef you think you kin trust your hide in Flat Crick school-house I ha'n't got no 'bjection. But ef you git licked don't come on us. Flat Crick don't pay no 'nsurance, you bet! Any other trustees? Wal, yes. But as I pay the most taxes, t'others jist let me run the thing. You can begin right off a Monday. They a'n't been no other applications. You see it takes some grit to apply for this school. The last master had a black eye for a month. But, as I said, you can jist roll up and wade in. I 'low you've got pluck, may be, and that goes for a heap sight more'n sinnoo with boys. Walk in, and stay over Sunday with me. You'll hev to board roun', and I guess you better begin here."

Ralph did not go in, but sat out on the wheelbarrow, watching the old man shave shingles, while the boys split the blocks and chopped wood. Bull smelled of the new-comer again in an ugly way, and got a good kick from the older son for his pains. But out of one of his red eyes the dog warned the young school-master that *he* should yet suffer for all kicks received on his account.

"Ef Bull once takes a holt, heaven and yarth can't make him let go," said the older son to Ralph, by way of comfort.

It was well for Ralph that he began to "board round" by stopping at Mr. Means's. Ralph felt that Flat Creek was what he needed. He had lived a bookish life. But here was his lesson in the art of managing people. For who can manage the untamed and strapping youths of a winter school in Hoopole County has gone far toward learning one of the hardest of lessons. And twenty-five years ago, in Ralph's time, things were worse than they are now.

The older son of Mr. Means was called Bud Means. What his real name was Ralph could not find out, for in many of these families the nickname of "Bud" given to the oldest boy, and that of "Sis" which is the birthright of the oldest girl, completely bury the proper Christian name. Ralph was a general. He saw his first strategic point, which was to capture Bud Means.

After supper the boys began to get ready for something. Bull stuck up his ears in a dignified way, and the three or four yellow curs who were Bull's satellites yelped delightedly and discordantly.

"Bill," said Bud Means to his brother, "ax the master ef he'd like to hunt coons. I'd like to take the starch out the stuck-up fellow."

" 'Nough said," was Bill's reply.

"You durn't do it," said Bud.

"I don't take no sech a dare," returned Bill, and walked down to the gate, on which Ralph stood watching the stars come out, and wishing he had never seen Flat Creek.

"I say, mister," began Bill, "mister, they's a coon what's been a eatin' our chickens lately, and we're goin' to try ketch the varmint. You wouldn't like to take a coon hunt nor nothin', would you?"

"Why, yes," said Ralph, "there's nothing I should like better, if I could only be sure Bull wouldn't mistake me for the coon."

And so, as a matter of policy, Ralph dragged his tired legs eight or ten miles, on hill and in hollow, after Bud, and Bill, and Bull, and the coon. But the raccoon climbed a tree. The boys got into a quarrel about whose business it was to have brought the ax, and who was to blame that the tree could not be felled. Now, if there was anything Ralph's muscles were good for, it was to climb. So, asking Bud to give him a start, he soon reached the limb above the one on which the raccoon was. Ralph did not know how ugly a customer a raccoon can be, and so got credit for more courage than he had. With much peril to his legs from the raccoon's teeth, he succeeded in shaking the poor creature off among the yelping brutes and yelling boys. Ralph could not help sympathizing with the hunted animal, which sold its life as dearly as possible, giving the dogs many a scratch and bite. It seemed to him that

4

he was like the raccoon, precipitated into the midst of a party of dogs who would rejoice in worrying *his* life out, as Bull and his crowd were destroying the poor raccoon. When Bull at last seized the raccoon and put an end to it, Ralph could not but admire the decided way in which he did it, calling to mind Bud's comment: "Ef Bull once takes a holt, heaven and yarth can't make him let go."

But as they walked home, Bud carrying the raccoon by the tail, Ralph felt that his hunt had not been in vain. He fancied that even red-eyed Bull, walking uncomfortably close to his heels, respected him more since he had climbed that tree.

"Purty peart kind of a master," remarked the old man to Bud after Ralph had gone to bed. "Guess you better be a little easy on *him*. Hey?"

But Bud deigned no reply. Perhaps because he knew that Ralph heard the conversation through the thin partition.

Ralph woke delighted to find it raining. He did not want to hunt or fish on Sunday, and this steady rain would enable him to make friends with Bud. I do not know how he got started, but after breakfast he began to tell stories. Out of all the books he had ever read he told story after story. And "old man Means," and "old *Miss* Means," and Bud Means, and Bill Means, and Sis Means, listened with great eyes while he told of Sinbad's adventures, of the Old Man of the Sea, of Robinson Crusoe, of Captain Gulliver's experiences in Liliput, and of Baron Munchausen's exploits.

Ralph had caught his fish. The hungry minds of these backwoods people, sick and dying of their own commonplace, were refreshed with the new life that came to their imaginations in these stories. For there was but one

5

book in the Means library, and that, a well-thumbed copy of Captain Riley's Narrative, had long since lost all freshness.

"I'll be dog-on'd," said Bill emphatically, "ef I hadn't ruther hear the master tell them whoppin' yarns, than to go to a circus the best day I ever seed!" Bill could pay no higher compliment.

What Ralph wanted was to make a friend of Bud. It's a nice thing to have the seventy-four-gun ship on your own side, and the more Hartsook admired the knotted muscles of Bud Means, the more he desired to attach him to himself. So, whenever he struck out a peculiarly brilliant passage, he anxiously watched Bud's eye. But the young Philistine kept his own counsel. He listened but said nothing, and the eyes under his shaggy brow gave no sign. Ralph could not tell whether those eyes were deep and inscrutable, or only stolid. Perhaps a little of both. When Monday morning came Ralph was nervous. He walked to school with Bud.

"I guess you're a little skeered by what the old man said, a'n't you?"

Ralph was about to deny it, but on reflection concluded that it was always best to speak the truth. He said that Mr. Means's description of the school had made him feel a little downhearted.

"What will you do with the tough boys? You a'n't no match for 'em." And Ralph felt Bud's eyes not only measuring his muscles, but scrutinizing his countenance. He only answered:

"I don't know."

"What would you do with me, for instance?" and Bud stretched himself up as if to shake out the reserve power coiled up in his great muscles.

"I shan't have any trouble with you."

6

"Why, I'm the worst chap of all. I thrashed the last master myself."

And again the eyes of Bud Means looked out sharply from his shadowing brows to see the effect of this speech on the slender young man.

"You won't thrash me, though," said Ralph.

"Pshaw! I 'low I could whip you in an inch of your life with my left hand and never half try," said young Means with a threatening sneer.

"I know that as well as you do."

"Well, a'n't you afraid of me then?" and again he looked sidewise at Ralph.

"Not a bit," said Ralph, wondering at his own courage.

They walked on in silence a minute. Bud was turning the matter over.

"Why a'n't you afraid of me?" he said presently.

"Because you and I are going to be friends."

"And what about t'others?"

"I am not afraid of all the other boys put together."

"You a'n't! The mischief! How's that?"

"Well, I'm not afraid of them because you and I are going to be friends, and you can whip all of them together. You'll do the fighting and I'll do the teaching."

The diplomatic Bud only chuckled a little at this; whether he assented to the alliance or not Ralph could not tell.

When Ralph looked round on the faces of the scholars —the little faces full of mischief and curiosity, the big faces full of an expression which was not further removed than second-cousin from contempt—when young Hartsook looked into these faces, his heart palpitated with stage-fright. There is no audience so hard to face as one of school children, as many a man has found to his cost. Perhaps it is that no conventional restraint can keep

7

down their laughter when you do or say anything ridiculous.

Hartsook's first day was hurried and unsatisfactory. He was not master of himself, and consequently not master of anybody else. When evening came there were symptoms of insubordination through the whole school. Poor Ralph was sick at heart. He felt that if there had ever been the shadow of an alliance between himself and Bud, it was all "off" now. It seemed to Hartsook that even Bull had lost his respect for the teacher. Half that night the young man lay awake. At last comfort came to him. A reminiscence of the death of the raccoon flashed on him like a vision. He remembered that quiet and annihilating bite which Bull gave. He remembered Bud's certificate, that "Ef Bull once takes a holt, heaven and yarth can't make him let go." He thought that what Flat Creek needed was a bull-dog. He would be a bull-dog, quiet but invincible. He would take hold in such a way that nothing should make him let go. And then he went to sleep.

In the morning Ralph got out of bed slowly. He put his clothes on slowly. He pulled on his boots in a bull-dog mood. He tried to move as he thought Bull would move if he were a man. He ate with deliberation, and looked everybody in the eyes with a manner that made Bud watch him curiously. He found himself continually comparing himself with Bull. He found Bull possessing a strange fascination for him. He walked to school alone, the rest having gone on before. He entered the school room preserving a cool and dogged manner. He saw in the eyes of the boys that there was mischief brewing. He did not dare sit down in his chair for fear of a pin.

Everybody looked solemn. Ralph lifted the lid of his desk. "Bow-wow! wow-wow!" It was the voice of an im-

8

prisoned puppy, and the school giggled and then roared. Then everything was quiet.

The scholars expected an outburst of wrath from the teacher. For they had come to regard the whole world as divided into two classes, the teacher on the one side representing lawful authority, and the pupils on the other in a state of chronic rebellion. To play a trick on the master was an evidence of spirit; to "lick" the master was to be the crowned hero of Flat Creek district. Such a hero was Bud Means, and Bill, who had less muscle, saw a chance to distinguish himself on a teacher of slender frame. Hence the puppy in the desk.

Ralph Hartsook grew red in the face when he saw the puppy. But the cool, repressed, bull-dog mood in which he had kept himself saved him. He lifted the dog into his arms and stroked him until the laughter subsided. Then, in a solemn and set way, he began:

"I am sorry," and he looked round the room with a steady, hard eye—everybody felt that there was a conflict coming—"I am sorry that any scholar in this school could be so mean"—the word was uttered with a sharp emphasis, and all the big boys felt sure that there would be a fight with Bill Means, and perhaps with Bud—"could be so *mean*—as to—shut up his *brother* in such a place as that!"

There was a long, derisive laugh. The wit was indifferent, but by one stroke Ralph had carried the whole school to his side. By the significant glances of the boys, Hartsook detected the perpetrator of the joke, and with the hard and dogged look in his eyes, with just such a look as Bull would give a puppy, but with the utmost suavity in his voice, he said:

"William Means, will you be so good as to put this dog out of doors?"

9

II

A Spell Coming

There was a moment of utter stillness. But the magnetism of Ralph's eye was too much for Bill Means. The request was so polite, the master's look was so innocent and yet so determined. Bill often wondered afterward that he had not "fit" rather than obeyed the request. But somehow he put the dog out. He was partly surprised, partly inveigled, partly awed into doing just what he had not intended to do. In the week that followed, Bill had to fight half a dozen boys for calling him "Puppy Means." Bill said he wished he'd a licked the master on the spot. 'Twould a saved five fights out of the six.

And all that day and the next, the bull-dog in the master's eye was a terror to evil-doers. At the close of school on the second day Bud was heard to give it as his opinion that "the master wouldn't be much in a tussle, but he had a heap of thunder and lightning in him." Did he inflict corporal punishment? inquires some philanthropic friend. Would you inflict corporal punishment if you were tiger-trainer in Van Amburgh's happy family? If you had been among the human bears on Flat Creek you would have used the rod also. But poor Ralph could never satisfy his constituency.

"Don't believe he'll do," was Mr. Pete Jones's comment to Mr. Means. "Don't thrash enough. Boys won't larn 'less you thrash 'em, says I. Leastways, mine won't. Lay it on good, is what I says to a master. Lay it on good. Don't do no harm. Lickin' and larnin' goes together. No lickin', no larnin', says I. Lickin' and larnin', lickin' and larnin', is the good ole way."

And Mr. Jones, like some wiser people, was the more pleased with his formula that it had an alliterative sound. Nevertheless, Ralph was master from this time until the spelling-school came. If only it had not been for that spelling-school! Many and many a time after the night of the fatal spelling-school Ralph used to say: "If only it had not been for that spelling-school!"

There had to be a spelling-school. Not only for the sake of my story, which would not have been worth the telling if the spelling-school had not taken place, but because Flat Creek district had to have a spelling-school. It is the only public literary exercise known in Hoopole County. It takes the place of lyceum lecture and debating club. Sis Means, or, as she wished now to be called, Mirandy Means, expressed herself most positively in favor of it. She said that she 'lowed the folks in that district couldn't in no wise do without it. But it was rather to its social than its intellectual benefits that she referred. For all the spelling-schools ever seen could not enable her to stand anywhere but at the foot of the class. There is one branch diligently taught in a backwoods school. The public mind seems impressed with the difficulties of English orthography, and there is a solemn conviction that the chief end of man is to learn to spell. " 'Know Webster's Elementary' came down from heaven," would be the backwoods version of the Greek proverb, but that, unfortunately for the Greeks, their fame has not reached so far. It often happens that the pupil does not know the meaning of a single word in the lesson. That is of no consequence. What do you want to know the meaning of a word for? Words were made to be spelled, and men were

11

created that they might spell them. Hence the necessity for sending a pupil through the spelling-book five times before you allow him to begin to read, or indeed to do anything else. Hence the necessity for those long spelling-classes at the close of each forenoon and afternoon session of the school, to stand at the head of which is the cherished ambition of every scholar. Hence, too, the necessity for devoting the whole of the afternoon session of each Friday to a "Spelling Match." In fact, spelling is the "national game" in Hoopole County. Base-ball and croquet matches are as unknown as Olympian chariot-races. Spelling and "shucking" are the only public competitions.

So that the fatal spelling-school had to be appointed for the Wednesday of the second week of the session, just when Ralph felt himself master of the situation. Not that he was without his annoyances. One of Ralph's troubles in the week before the spelling school was that he was loved. The other that he was hated. And while the time between the appointing of the spelling tournament and the actual occurrence of that remarkable event is engaged in elapsing, let me narrate two incidents that made it for Ralph a trying time.

III

Mirandy, Hank, and Shocky

Mirandy had nothing but contempt for the new master until he developed the bull-dog in his character. Mirandy fell in love with the bull-dog. Like many other girls of her class, she was greatly enamored with the "subjection of women," and she stood ready to fall in love with any man strong enough to be her master. Much has been said of the strong-minded women. I offer this psychological remark as a contribution to the natural history of the weak-minded women.

It was at the close of that very second day on which Ralph had achieved his first victory over the school, and in which Mirandy had been seized with her desperate passion for him, that she told him about it. Not in words. We do not allow *that* in the most civilized countries, and it would not be tolerated in Hoopole County. But Mirandy told the master the fact that she was in love with him none the less that no word passed her lips. She walked by him from school. She cast at him what are commonly called sheep's-eyes. Ralph thought them more like calf's-eyes. She changed the whole tone of her voice. She whined ordinarily. Now she whimpered. And so by ogling him, by blushing at him, by tittering at him, by giggling at him, by snickering at him, by simpering at him, by making herself tenfold more a fool even than nature had made her, she managed to convey to the dismayed soul of the young teacher the frightful intelligence that

13

he was loved by the richest, the ugliest, the silliest, the coarsest, and the most entirely contemptible girl in Flat Creek district.

Ralph sat by the fire the next morning trying to read a few minutes before school-time, while the boys were doing the chores, and the bound girl was milking the cows, with no one in the room but the old woman. She was generally as silent as Bud, but now she seemed for some unaccountable reason disposed to talk. She had sat down on the broad hearth to have her usual morning smoke; the poplar table, adorned by no cloth, sat in the floor; the unwashed blue tea-cups sat in the unwashed blue saucers; the unwashed blue plates kept company with the begrimed blue pitcher. The dirty skillets by the fire were kept in countenance by the dirtier pots, and the ashes were drifted and strewn over the hearth-stones in a most picturesque way.

"You see," said the old woman, knocking the residuum from her cob-pipe, and chafing some dry leaf between her withered hands preparatory to filling it again, "you see Mr. Hartsook, my ole man's purty well along in the world. He's got a right smart lot of this world's plunder one way and another." And while she stuffed the tobacco in her pipe Ralph wondered why she should mention it to him. "You see we moved in here nigh upon twenty-five year ago. 'Twas when my Jack, him as died afore Bud was born, was a baby. Bud'll be twenty-one the fifth of next June."

Here Mrs. Means stopped to rake a live coal out of the fire with her skinny finger, and then to carry it in her skinny palm to the bowl—or to the *hole*—of her cob-pipe. When she got the smoke agoing she proceeded:

"You see this ere bottom land was all Congress land in them there days, and it sold for a dollar and a quarter

14

and I says to my ole man, 'Jack,' says I, 'Jack, do you git a plenty while you're a gittin'. Git a plenty while you're a gittin',' says I, 'fer 'twon't never be no cheaper'n 'tis now,' and it ha'n't been, I knowed 'twouldn't,'" and Mrs. Means took the pipe from her mouth to indulge in a good chuckle at the thought of her financial shrewdness. "'Git a plenty while you're a gittin',' says I. I could see, you know, they was a powerful sight of money in Congress land. That's what made me say, 'Git a plenty while you're a gittin'.' And Jack, he's wuth lots and gobs of money, all made out of Congress land. Jack didn't git rich by hard work. Bless you, no! Not him. That a'n't his way. Hard work a'n't, you know. 'Twas that air six hundred dollars he got along of me, all salted down into Flat Crick bottoms at a dollar and a quarter a acre, and 'twas my sayin' 'Git a plenty while you're a gittin' ' as done it." And here the old ogre laughed, or grinned horribly, at Ralph, showing her few straggling, discolored teeth.

Then she got up and knocked the ashes out of her pipe, and laid the pipe away and walked round in front of Ralph. After adjusting the "chunks" so that the fire would burn, she turned her yellow face toward Ralph, and scanning him closely came out with the climax of her speech in the remark: "You see as how, Mr. Hartsook, the man what gits my Mirandy'll do well. Flat Crick land's worth nigh upon a hundred a acre."

This gentle hint came near knocking Ralph down. Had Flat Creek land been worth a hundred times a hundred dollars an acre, and had he owned five hundred times Means's five hundred acres, he would have given it all just at that moment to have annihilated the whole tribe of Meanses. Except Bud. Bud was a giant, but a good-natured one. He thought he would except Bud from the general destruction. As for the rest, he mentally pictured to himself the pleasure of attending their funerals. There was one thought, however, between him and despair. He felt confident that the cordiality, the intensity, and the persistency of his dislike of Sis Means were such that he should never inherit a foot of the Flat Creek bottoms.

But what about Bud? What if he joined the conspiracy to marry him to this weak-eyed, weak-headed wood nymph, or backwoods nymph?

If Ralph felt it a misfortune to be loved by Mirandy Means, he found himself almost equally unfortunate in having incurred the hatred of the meanest boy in school. "Hank" Banta, low-browed, smirky, and crafty, was the first sufferer by Ralph's determination to use corporal punishment, and so Henry Banta, who was a compound of deceit and resentment, never lost an opportunity to annoy the young school-master, who was obliged to live perpetually on his guard against his tricks.

One morning, as Ralph walked toward the school house, he met little Shocky. What the boy's first name or last name was the teacher did not know. He had given his name as Shocky, and all the teacher knew was that he was commonly called Shocky, that he was an orphan, that he lived with a family named Pearson over in Rocky Hollow, and that he was the most faithful and affectionate child in the school. On this morning that I speak of, Ralph had walked toward the school early to avoid the company of Mirandy. But not caring to sustain his dignity longer than was necessary, he loitered along the road admiring the trunks of the maples, and picking up a beech-nut now and then. Just as he was about to go on toward the school, he caught sight of little Shocky running swiftly toward him, but looking from side to side, as if afraid of being seen.

"Well, Shocky, what is it?" and Ralph put his hand

kindly on the great bushy head of white hair from which came Shocky's nickname. Shocky had to pant a minute.

"Why, Mr. Hartsook," he gasped, scratching his head, "they's a pond down underneath the school-house," and here Shocky's breath gave out entirely for a minute.

"Yes, Shocky, I know that. What about it? The trustees haven't come to fill it up, have they?"

"Oh! no, sir; but Hank Banta, you know—" and Shocky took another breathing spell, standing as close to Ralph as he could, for poor Shocky got all his sunshine from the master's presence.

"Has Henry fallen in and got a ducking, Shocky?"

"Oh! no, sir; he wants to git you in, you see."

"Well, I won't go in, though, Shocky."

"But, you see, he's been and gone and pulled back the board that you have to step on to git ahind your desk; he's been and gone and pulled back the board so as you can't help a-tippin' it up, and a-sowsin' right in ef you step there."

"And so you came to tell me." There was a huskiness in Ralph's voice. He had, then, one friend in Flat Creek district—poor little Shocky. He put his arm around Shocky just a moment, and then told him to hasten across to the other road, so as to come back to the school-house in a direction at right angles to the master's approach. But the caution was not needed. Shocky had taken care to leave in that way, and was altogether too cunning to be seen coming down the road with Mr. Hartsook. But after he got over the fence to go through the "sugar camp" (or sugar *orchard*, as they say at the East), he stopped and turned back once or twice, just to catch one more smile from Ralph. And then he hied away through the tall trees a very happy boy, kicking and plowing the brown leaves before him in his perfect delight, saying over and over again, "How he looked at me! how he did look!" And when Ralph came up to the school-house door, there was Shocky sauntering along from the other direction, throwing bits of limestone at fence-rails, and smiling still clear down to his shoes at thought of the master's kind words.

"What a quare boy Shocky is!" remarked Betsey Short, with a giggle. "He just likes to wander 'round alone. I see him a-comin' out of the sugar camp just now. He's been in there half an hour." And Betsey giggled again. For Betsey Short could giggle on slighter provocation than any other girl on Flat Creek.

When Ralph Hartsook, with the quiet, dogged tread that he was cultivating, walked into the school-room, he took great care not to seem to see the trap set for him. But he carelessly stepped over the board that had been so nicely adjusted. The boys who were Hank's confidants in the plot were very busy over their slates, and took pains not to show their disappointment.

The morning session wore on without incident. Ralph several times caught two people looking at him. One was Mirandy. Her weak and watery eyes stole loving glances over the top of her spelling-book, which she would not study. Her looks always made Ralph's spirits sink to forty below zero, and congeal.

But on one of the backless little benches that sat in the middle of the school-room was little Shocky, who also cast many love-glances at the young master, glances as grateful to his heart as Mirandy's ogling—he was tempted to call it ogring—was hateful.

"Look at Shocky," giggled Betsey Short, behind her slate. "He looks as if he was a-goin' to eat the master up, body and soul."

It is safe to conjecture that Betsey had never studied

Drew on the Immateriality and Immortality of the Human Soul," or she would not have spoken of Ralph's as it were something to be swallowed like an oyster.

And so the forenoon wore on as usual, and those who had laid the trap had forgotten it themselves. The morning session was drawing to a close. The fire in the great, old fire-place had burnt low. The flames, which seemed to Shocky to be angels, had disappeared, and now the bright coals, which had played the part of men and women and houses in Shocky's fancy, had taken on a white and downy covering of ashes, and the great half-burnt back-log lay there smoldering like a giant asleep in a snow-drift. Shocky longed to wake him up.

As for Henry Banta, he was too much bothered to get the answer to a "sum" he was doing, to remember anything about his trap. In fact, he had quite forgotten that half an hour ago in the all-absorbing employment of drawing ugly pictures on his slate and coaxing Betsey Short to giggle by showing them slily across the school-room. Once or twice Ralph had been attracted to Betsey's extraordinary fits of giggling, and had come so near to catching Hank that the boy thought it best not to run any farther risk of the beech switches, four or five feet long, laid up behind the master in sight of the school as a prophylactic. Hence his application just now to his sum in long division, and hence his puzzled look, for, idler that he was, his "sums" did not solve themselves easily. As usual in such cases, he came up in front of the master's desk to have the difficulty explained. He had to wait a minute until Ralph got through with showing Betsey Short, who had been seized with a studying fit, and who could hardly give any attention to the teacher's explanations, she did want to giggle so much! Not at anything in particular, but just at things in general.

19

While Ralph was "doing" Betsey's sum for her, he was solving a much more difficult question. A plan had flashed upon him, but the punishment seemed a severe one. He gave it up once or twice, but he remembered how turbulent the Flat Creek elements were; and had he not only resolved to be as unrelenting as a bull-dog? He fortified himself by recalling again the oft-remembered remark of Bud, "Ef Bull wunst takes a holt, heaven and yarth can't make him let go." And so he resolved to give Hank and the whole school one good lesson.

"Just step round behind me, Henry, and you can see how I do this," said Ralph.

Hank was entirely off his guard, and with his eyes fixed upon the slate on the teacher's desk, he sidled round upon the broad loose board, misplaced by his own hand, and in an instant the other end of the board rose up in the middle of the school-room, almost striking Shocky in the face, while Henry Banta brought up or down in the ice-cold water beneath the school-house.

"Why, Henry!" cried Ralph, jumping to his feet with well-feigned surprise. "How *did* this happen?" and he helped the dripping fellow out and seated him by the fire.

Betsey Short giggled.

Shocky was so tickled that he could hardly keep his seat.

The boys who were in the plot looked very serious indeed. And a little silly.

Ralph made some remarks by way of improving the occasion. He spoke strongly of the utter meanness of the one who could play so heartless a trick on a schoolmate. He said that it was as much thieving to get your fun at the expense of another as to steal his money. And while he talked all eyes were turned on Hank. All except the eyes of Mirandy Means. They looked simperingly at Ralph. All the rest looked at Hank. The fire had made his face very red. Shocky noticed that. Betsey Short noticed it, and giggled. The master wound up with an appropriate quotation from Scripture. He said that the person who displaced that board had better not be encouraged by the success—he said *success* with a curious emphasis—of the present experiment to attempt another trick of the kind. For it was set down in the Bible that if a man dug a pit for the feet of another he would be very likely to fall in it himself. Which made all the pupils look solemn. Except Betsey Short. She giggled. And Shocky wanted to. And Mirandy cast an expiring look at Ralph. And if the teacher was not love-sick, he certainly was sick of Mirandy's love.

When school was "let out" Ralph gave Hank every caution that he could about taking cold, and even lent him his overcoat, very much against Hank's will. For Hank had obstinately refused to go home before the school was dismissed.

Then the master walked out in a quiet and subdued way to spend the noon recess in the woods, while Shocky watched his retreating footsteps with loving admiration. And the pupils not in the secret canvassed the question of who moved the board. Bill Means said he'd bet Hank did it, which set Betsey Short off in an uncontrollable giggle. And Shocky listened innocently.

But that night Bud said slily, "Thunder and lightning! what a manager you *air*, Mr. Hartsook!" To which Ralph returned no reply except a friendly smile. Muscle paid tribute to brains that time.

But Ralph had no time for exultation. For just here came the spelling-school.

IV

Spelling Down the Master

"I 'low," said Mrs. Means, as she stuffed the tobacco into
her cob pipe after supper on that eventful Wednesday
evening, "I 'low they'll appint the Squire to gin out the
words to-night. They mos' always do, you see, kase he's
the peartest *ole* man in this deestrick; and I 'low some
of the young fellers would have to git up and dust ef they
would keep up to him. And he uses sech remarkable
smart words. He speaks so polite, too. But laws! don't
I remember when he was poarer nor Job's turkey?
Twenty year ago, when he come to these 'ere diggins,
that air Squire Hawkins was a poar Yankee school-
master, that said 'pail' instid of bucket, and that called a
cow a 'caow,' and that couldn't tell to save his gizzard
what we meant by *'low* and by *right smart*. But he's
larnt our ways now, an' he's jest as civilized as the rest
of us. You would-n know he'd ever been a Yankee. He
didn't stay poar long. Not he. He jest married a right
rich girl! He! he!" and the old woman grinned at Ralph,
and then at Mirandy, and then at the rest, until Ralph
shuddered. Nothing was so frightful to him as to be
fawned on and grinned at by this old ogre, whose few
lonesome, blackish teeth seemed ready to devour him.
"He didn't stay poar, you bet a hoss!" and with this the
coal was deposited on the pipe, and the lips began to
crack like parchment as each puff of smoke escaped. "He
married rich, you see," and here another significant look

t the young master, and another fond look at Mirandy, as
he puffed away reflectively. "His wife hadn't no book-
arnin'. She'd been through the spellin'-book wunst, and
had got as fur as 'asperity' on it a second time. But she
couldn't read a word when she was married, and never
ould. She warn't overly smart. She hadn't hardly got the
ense the law allows. But schools was skase in them air
days, and, besides, book-larnin' don't do no good to a
woman. Makes her stuck up. I never knowed but one gal
in my life as had ciphered into fractions, and she was
o dog-on stuck up that she turned up her nose one night
at a apple-peelin' bekase I tuck a sheet off the bed to
plice out the table-cloth, which was ruther short. And
he sheet was mos' clean, too. Had-n been slep on more'n
wunst or twicet. But I was goin' fer to say that when
Squire Hawkins married Virginny Gray he got a heap o'
money, or, what's the same thing mostly, a heap o' good
land. And that's better'n book-larnin', says I. Ef a girl had
gone clean through all eddication, and got to the rule of
hree itself, that would-n buy a feather-bed. Squire
Hawkins jest put eddication agin the gal's farm, and
traded even, an' ef ary one of 'em got swindled, I never
heerd no complaints."

And here she looked at Ralph in triumph, her hard face
splintering into the hideous semblance of a smile. And Mirandy cast a blushing, gushing, all-imploring, and all-
confiding look on the young master.

"I say, ole woman," broke in old Jack, "I say, wot is all
this ere spoutin' about the Square fer?" and old Jack,
having bit off an ounce of "pigtail," returned the plug to
his pocket.

As for Ralph, he wanted to die. He had a guilty feeling
that this speech of the old lady's had somehow committed him beyond recall to Mirandy. He did not see visions

of breach-of-promise suits. But he trembled at the thought of an avenging big brother.

"Hanner, you kin come along, too, ef you're a mind, when you git the dishes washed," said Mrs. Means to the bound girl, as she shut and latched the back door. The Means family had built a new house in front of the old one, as a sort of advertisement of bettered circumstances, an eruption of shoddy feeling; but when the new building was completed, they found themselves unable to occupy it for anything else than a lumber-room, and so, except a parlor which Mirandy had made an effort to furnish a little (in hope of the blissful time when somebody should "set up" with her of evenings), the new building was almost unoccupied, and the family went in and out through the back door, which, indeed, was the front door also, for, according to a curious custom, the "front" of the house was placed toward the south, though the "big road" (Hoosier for *highway*) ran along the north-west side, or, rather, past the north-west corner of it.

When the old woman had spoken thus to Hannah and had latched the door, she muttered, "That gal don't never show no gratitude fer favors"; to which Bud rejoined that he didn't think she had no great sight to be pertickler thankful fer. To which Mrs. Means made no reply, thinking it best, perhaps, not to wake up her dutiful son on so interesting a theme as her treatment of Hannah. Ralph felt glad that he was this evening to go to another boarding place. He should not hear the rest of the controversy.

Ralph walked to the school-house with Bill. They were friends again. For when Hank Banta's ducking and his dogged obstinacy in sitting in his wet clothes had brought on a serious fever, Ralph had called together the big boys, and had said: "We must take care of one another, boys. Who will volunteer to take turns sitting up with

24

Henry?" He put his own name down, and all the rest followed.

"William Means and myself will sit up to-night," said Ralph. And poor Bill had been from that moment the teacher's friend. He was chosen to be Ralph's companion. He was Puppy Means no longer! Hank could not be conquered by kindness, and the teacher was made to feel the bitterness of his resentment long after, as we shall find. But Bill Means was for the time entirely placated, and he and Ralph went to spelling-school together.

Every family furnished a candle. There were yellow dips and white dips, burning, smoking, and flaring. There was laughing, and talking, and giggling, and simpering, and ogling, and flirting, and courting. What a dress party is to Fifth Avenue, a spelling-school is to Hoopole County. It is an occasion which is metaphorically inscribed with this legend, "Choose your partners." Spelling is only a blind in Hoopole County, as is dancing on Fifth Avenue. But as there are some in society who love dancing for its own sake, so in Flat Creek district there were those who loved spelling for its own sake, and who, smelling the battle from afar, had come to try their skill in this tournament, hoping to freshen the laurels they had won in their school-days.

"I 'low," said Mr. Means, speaking as the principal school trustee, "I 'low our friend the Square is jest the man to boss this ere consarn to-night. Ef nobody objects, I'll appoint him. Come, Square, don't be bashful. Walk up to the trough, fodder or no fodder, as the man said to his donkey."

There was a general giggle at this, and many of the young swains took occasion to nudge the girls alongside them, ostensibly for the purpose of making them see the joke, but really for the pure pleasure of nudging. The

25

Greeks figured Cupid as naked, probably because he wears so many disguises that they could not select a costume for him.

The Squire came to the front. Ralph made an inventory of the agglomeration which bore the name of Squire Hawkins, as follows:

1. A swallow-tail coat of indefinite age, worn only on state occasions when its owner was called to figure in his public capacity. Either the Squire had grown too large or the coat too small.

2. A pair of black gloves, the most phenomenal, abnormal, and unexpected apparition conceivable in Flat Creek district, where the preachers wore no coats in the summer, and where a black glove was never seen except on the hands of the Squire.

3. A wig of that dirty, waxy color so common to wigs. This one showed a continual inclination to slip off the owner's smooth, bald pate, and the Squire had frequently to adjust it. As his hair had been red, the wig did not accord with his face, and the hair ungrayed was sadly discordant with a face shriveled by age.

4. A semicircular row of whiskers hedging the edge of the jaw and chin. These were dyed a frightful dead black, such as no natural hair or beard ever had. At the roots there was a quarter of an inch of white, giving the whiskers the appearance of having been stuck on.

5. A pair of spectacles "with tortoise-shell rim." Wont to slip off.

6. A glass eye, purchased of a peddler, and differing in color from its natural mate, perpetually getting out of focus by turning in or out.

7. A set of false teeth, badly fitted, and given to bobbing up and down.

8. The Squire proper, to whom these patches were loosely attached.

It is an old story that a boy wrote home to his father begging him to come West, because "mighty mean men got in office out here." But Ralph concluded that some Yankees had taught school in Hoopole County who would not have held a high place in the educational institutions of Massachusetts. Hawkins had some New England idioms, but they were well overlaid by a Western pronunciation.

"Ladies and gentlemen," he began, shoving up his spectacles, and sucking his lips over his white teeth to keep them in place, "ladies and gentlemen, young men and maidens, raley I'm obleeged to Mr. Means fer this honor," and the Squire took both hands and turned the top of his head round several inches. Then he adjusted his spectacles. Whether he was obliged to Mr. Means for the honor of being compared to a donkey, was not clear. "I feel in the inmost compartments of my animal spirits a most happifying sense of the success and futility of all my endeavors to sarve the people of Flat Crick deestrick, and the people of Tomkins township, in my weak way and manner." This burst of eloquence was delivered with a constrained air and an apparent sense of a danger that he, Squire Hawkins, might fall to pieces in his weak way and manner, and of the success and futility (especially the latter) of all attempts at reconstruction. For by this time the ghastly pupil of the left eye, which was black, was looking away round to the left, while the little blue one on the right twinkled cheerfully toward the front. The front teeth would drop down so that the Squire's mouth was kept nearly closed, and his words whistled through.

"I feel as if I could be grandiloquent on this interesting occasion," twisting his scalp round, "but raley I must forego any such exertions. It is spelling you want. Spelling is the corner-stone, the grand, underlying subterfuge of a good eddication. I put the spellin'-book prepared by the great Daniel Webster alongside the Bible. I do, raley. I think I may put it ahead of the Bible. For if it wurnt fer spellin'-books and sich occasions as these, where would the Bible be? I should like to know. The man who got up, who compounded this little work of inextricable valoo was a benufactor to the whole human race or any other." Here the spectacles fell off. The Squire replaced them in some confusion, gave the top of his head another twist, and felt of his glass eye, while poor Shocky stared in wonder, and Betsey Short rolled from side to side at the point of death from the effort to suppress her giggle. Mrs. Means and the other old ladies looked the applause they could not speak.

"I appint Larkin Lanham and Jeems Buchanan fer captings," said the Squire. And the two young men thus named took a stick and tossed it from hand to hand to decide which should have the "first choice." One tossed the stick to the other, who held it fast just where he happened to catch it. Then the first placed his hand above the second, and so the hands were alternately changed to the top. The one who held the stick last without room for the other to take hold had gained the lot. This was tried three times. As Larkin held the stick twice out of three times, he had the choice. He hesitated a moment. Everybody looked toward tall Jim Phillips. But Larkin was fond of a venture on unknown seas, and so he said, "I take the master," while a buzz of surprise ran round the room, and the captain of the other side, as if afraid his opponent would withdraw the choice, retorted quickly, and with a little smack of exultation and defiance in his voice: "And *I* take Jeems Phillips."

And soon all present, except a few of the old folks, found themselves ranged in opposing hosts, the poor spellers lagging in, with what grace they could, at the foot of the two divisions. The Squire opened his spelling-book and began to give out the words to the two captains, who stood up and spelled against each other. It was not long until Larkin spelled "really" with one *l*, and had to sit down in confusion, while a murmur of satisfaction ran through the ranks of the opposing forces. His own side bit their lips. The slender figure of the young teacher took the place of the fallen leader, and the excitement made the house very quiet. Ralph dreaded the loss of influence he would suffer if he should be easily spelled down. And at the moment of rising he saw in the darkest corner the figure of a well-dressed young man sitting in the shadow. It made him tremble. Why should his evil genius haunt him? But by a strong effort he turned his attention away from Dr. Small, and listened carefully to the words which the Squire did not pronounce very distinctly, spelling them with extreme deliberation. This gave him an air of hesitation which disappointed those on his own side. They wanted him to spell with a dashing assurance. But he did not begin a word until he had mentally felt his way through it. After ten minutes of spelling hard words Jeems Buchanan, the captain on the other side, spelled "atrocious" with an *s* instead of a *c*, and subsided, his first choice, Jeems Phillips, coming up against the teacher. This brought the excitement to fever-heat. For though Ralph was chosen first, it was entirely on trust, and most of the company were disappointed. The champion who now stood up against the school-master was a famous speller.

Jim Phillips was a tall, lank, stoop-shouldered fellow, who had never distinguished himself in any other pursuit than spelling. Except in this one art of spelling he was of no account. He could not catch well or bat well in ball. He could not throw well enough to make his mark in that famous Western game of bull-pen. He did not succeed well in any study but that of Webster's Elementary. But in that he was—to use the usual Flat Creek locution—in that he was "a hoss." This genius for spelling is in some people a sixth sense, a matter of intuition. Some spellers are born and not made, and their facility reminds one of the mathematical prodigies that crop out every now and then to bewilder the world. Bud Means, foreseeing that Ralph would be pitted against Jim Phillips, had warned his friend that Jim could "spell like thunder and lightning," and that it "took a powerful smart speller" to beat him, for he knew "a heap of spelling-book." To have "spelled down the master" is next thing to having whipped the biggest bully in Hoopole County, and Jim had "spelled down" the last three masters. He divided the hero-worship of the district with Bud Means.

For half an hour the Squire gave out hard words. What a blessed thing our crooked orthography is! Without it there could be no spelling-schools. As Ralph discovered his opponent's mettle he became more and more cautious. He was now satisfied that Jim would eventually beat him. The fellow evidently knew more about the spelling-book than old Noah Webster himself. As he stood there, with his dull face and long sharp nose, his hands behind his back, and his voice spelling infallibly, it seemed to Hartsook that his superiority must lie in his nose. Ralph's cautiousness answered a double purpose: it enabled him to tread surely, and it was mistaken by Jim for weakness. Phillips was now confident that he should carry off the calp of the fourth school-master before the evening was ̶ver. He spelled eagerly, confidently, brilliantly. Stoop-houldered as he was, he began to straighten up. In the ̶ninds of all the company the odds were in his favor. He ̶aw this, and became ambitious to distinguish himself ̶y spelling without giving the matter any thought.

Ralph always believed that he would have been speedily ̶efeated by Phillips had it not been for two thoughts ̶vhich braced him. The sinister shadow of young Dr. ̶mall sitting in the dark corner by the water-bucket ̶erved him. A victory over Phillips was a defeat to one ̶vho wished only ill to the young school-master. The other ̶hought that kept his pluck alive was the recollection of ̶ull. He approached a word as Bull approached the ̶accoon. He did not take hold until he was sure of his ̶ame. When he took hold, it was with a quiet assurance ̶f success. As Ralph spelled in this dogged way for half an ̶our the hardest words the Squire could find, the excite-̶ment steadily rose in all parts of the house, and Ralph's ̶riends even ventured to whisper that "may be Jim had ̶otched his match after all!"

But Phillips never doubted of his success.

"Theodolite," said the Squire.

"T-h-e, the, o-d, od, theod, o, theodo, l-y-t-e, theodo-̶ite," spelled the champion.

"Next," said the Squire, nearly losing his teeth in his ̶xcitement.

Ralph spelled the word slowly and correctly, and the conquered champion sat down in confusion. The excite-̶ment was so great for some minutes that the spelling was suspended. Everybody in the house had shown sympathy with one or the other of the combatants, except the silent shadow in the corner. *It* had not moved during the con-test, and did not show any interest now in the result.

"Gewhilliky crickets! Thunder and lightning! Licked him all to smash!" said Bud, rubbing his hands on his knees. "That beats my time all holler!"

And Betsey Short giggled until her tuck-comb fell out though she was on the defeated side.

Shocky got up and danced with pleasure.

But one suffocating look from the aqueous eyes of Mirandy destroyed the last spark of Ralph's pleasure in his triumph, and sent that awful below-zero feeling all through him.

"He's powerful smart, is the master," said old Jack to Mr. Pete Jones. "He'll beat the whole kit and tuck of 'em afore he's through. I know'd he was smart. That's the reason I tuck him," proceeded Mr. Means.

"Yaas, but he don't lick enough. Not nigh," answered Pete Jones. "No lickin', no larnin', says I."

It was now not so hard. The other spellers on the opposite side went down quickly under the hard words which the Squire gave out. The master had mowed down all but a few, his opponents had given up the battle and all had lost their keen interest in a contest to which there could be but one conclusion, for there were only the poor spellers left. But Ralph Hartsook ran against a stump where he was least expecting it. It was the Squire's custom, when one of the smaller scholars or poorer spellers rose to spell against the master, to give out eight or ten easy words that they might have some breathing spell before being slaughtered, and then to give a poser or two which soon settled them. He let them run a little as a cat does a doomed mouse. There was now but one person left on the opposite side, and as she rose in her blue calico dress, Ralph recognized Hannah, the bound girl at old Jack Means's. She had not attended school in the district, and had never spelled in spelling-school before, and was chosen last as an uncertain quantity. The Squire began with easy words of two syllables, from that page of Webster, so well known to all who ever thumbed it, as "Baker," from the word that stands at the top of the page. She spelled these words in an absent and un-interested manner. As everybody knew that she would have to go down as soon as this preliminary skirmishing was over, everybody began to get ready to go home, and already there was the buzz of preparation. Young men were timidly asking girls if "they could see them safe home," which is the approved formula, and were trem-bling in mortal fear of "the mitten." Presently the Squire, thinking it time to close the contest, pulled his scalp for-ward, adjusted his glass eye, which had been examining his long nose long enough, and turned over the leaves of the book to the great words at the place known to spellers as "Incomprehensibility," and began to give out those "words of eight syllables with the accent on the sixth." Listless scholars now turned round, and ceased to whis-per in order to be in at the master's final triumph. But to their surprise, "ole Miss Meanses' white nigger," as some of them called her, in allusion to her slavish life, spelled these great words with as perfect ease as the master. Still, not doubting the result, the Squire turned from place to place and selected all the hard words he could find. The school became utterly quiet, the excitement was too great for the ordinary buzz. Would "Meanses' Hanner" beat the master? Beat the master that had laid out Jim Phillips? Everybody's sympathy was now turned to Hannah. Ralph noticed that even Shocky had deserted him, and that his face grew brilliant every time Hannah spelled a word. In fact, Ralph deserted himself. As he saw the fine, timid face of the girl so long oppressed flush and shine with interest, as he looked at the rather

33

low but broad and intelligent brow and the fresh, white complexion, and saw the rich, womanly nature coming to the surface under the influence of applause and sympathy, he did not want to beat. If he had not felt that a victory given would insult her, he would have missed intentionally. The bull-dog, the stern, relentless setting of the will, had gone, he knew not whither. And there had come in its place, as he looked in that face, a something which he did not understand. You did not, gentle reader, the first time it came to you.

The Squire was puzzled. He had given out all the hard words in the book. He again pulled the top of his head forward. Then he wiped his spectacles and put them on. Then out of the depths of his pocket he fished up a list of words just coming into use in those days—words not in the spelling-book. He regarded the paper attentively with his blue right eye. His black left eye meanwhile fixed itself in such a stare on Mirandy Means that she shuddered and hid her eyes in her red silk handkerchief.

"Daguerreotype," sniffled the Squire. It was Ralph's turn.

"D-a-u, dau——"

"Next."

And Hannah spelled it right.

Such a buzz followed that Betsey Short's giggle could not be heard, but Shocky shouted, "Hanner beat! my Hanner spelled down the master!" And Ralph went over and congratulated her.

And Dr. Small sat perfectly still in the corner.

And then the Squire called them to order, and said: "As our friend Hanner Thomson is the only one left on her side, she will have to spell against nearly all on t'other side. I shall, therefore, take the liberty of procrastinating the completion of this interesting and exacting

34

contest until to-morrow evening. I hope our friend Hanner may again carry off the cypress crown of glory. There is nothing better for us than healthful and kindly simulation."

Dr. Small, who knew the road to practice, escorted Mirandy, and Bud went home with somebody else. The others of the Means family hurried on, while Hannah, the champion, stayed behind a minute to speak to Shocky. Perhaps it was because Ralph saw that Hannah must go alone that he suddenly remembered having left something which was of no consequence, and resolved to go round by Mr. Means's and get it. Another of Cupid's disguises.

V

The Walk Home

You expect me to describe that walk. You have had enough of the Jack Meanses and the Squire Hawkinses, and the Pete Joneses, and the rest. You wish me to tell you now of this true-hearted girl and her lover; of how the silvery moonbeams came down in a shower—to use Whittier's favorite metaphor—through the maple boughs, flecking the frozen ground with light and shadow. You would have me tell of the evening star, not yet gone down, which shed its benediction on them. But I shall do no such thing. For the moon was not shining, neither did the stars give their light. The tall black trunks of the maples swayed and shook in the wind, which moaned through their leafless boughs. Novelists always make lovers walk in the moonlight. But if love is not, as the cynics believe, all moonshine, it can at least make its own light. Moonlight is never so little needed or heeded, never so much of an impertinence, as in a love-scene. It was at the bottom of the first hollow beyond the school-house that Ralph overtook the timid girl walking swiftly through the dark. He did not ask permission to walk with her. Love does not go by words, and there are times when conventionality is impossible. There are people who understand one another at once. When one Soul meets another, it is not by pass-word, nor by hailing sign, nor by mysterious grip, that they recognize. The subtlest freemasonry in the world is this freemasonry of the spirit.

Ralph and Hannah knew and trusted. Ralph had admired and wondered at the quiet drudge. But it was when, in the unaccustomed sunshine of praise, she spread her wings a little, that he loved her. He had seen her awake.

You, Miss Amelia, wish me to repeat all their love-talk. I am afraid you'd find it dull. Love can pipe through any kind of a reed. Ralph talked love to Hannah when he spoke of the weather, of the crops, of the spelling-school. Weather, crops, and spelling-school—these were what his words would say if reported. But below all these commonplaces there vibrated something else. One can make love a great deal better when one doesn't speak of love. Words are so poor! Tones and modulations are better. It is an old story that Whitefield could make an audience weep by his way of pronouncing the word Mesopotamia. A lover can sound the whole gamut of his affection in saying Good morning. The solemnest engagements ever made have been without the intervention of speech.

And you, my Gradgrind friend, you think me sentimental. Two young fools they were, walking so slowly though the night was sharp, dallying under the trees, and dreaming of a heaven they could not have realized if all their wishes had been granted. Of course they were fools! Either they were fools to be so happy, or else some other people are fools not to be. After all, dear Gradgrind, let them be. There's no harm in it. They'll get trouble enough before morning. Let them enjoy the evening. I am not sure but these lovers whom we write down fools are the only wise people after all. Is it not wise to be happy? Let them alone.

For the first time in three years, for the first time since she had crossed the threshold of "Old Jack Means" and come under the domination of Mrs. Old Jack Means,

Hannah talked cheerfully, almost gaily. It was something to have a companion to talk to. It was something to be the victor even in a spelling-match, and to be applauded even by Flat Creek. And so, chatting earnestly about the most uninteresting themes, Ralph courteously helped Hannah over the fence, and they took the usual short-cut through the "blue-grass pasture." There came up a little shower, hardly more than a sprinkle, but then it was so nice to have a shower just as they reached the box-elder tree by the spring! It was so thoughtful in Ralph to suggest that the shade of a box-elder is dense, and that Hannah might take cold! And it was so easy for Hannah to yield to the suggestion. Just as though she had not milked the cows in the open lot in the worst storms of the last three years! And just as though the house were not within a stone's throw! Doubtless it was not prudent to stop there. But let us deal gently with them. Who would not stay in paradise ten minutes longer, even though it did make purgatory the hotter afterward? And so Hannah stayed.

"Tell me your circumstances," said Ralph, at last. "I am sure I can help you in something."

"No, no! you can not," and Hannah's face was clouded. "No one can help me. Only time and God. I must go, Mr. Hartsook." And they walked on to the front gate in silence and in some constraint. But still in happiness.

As they came to the gate, Dr. Small pushed past them in his cool, deliberate way, and mounted his horse. Ralph bade Hannah good-night, having entirely forgotten the errand which had been his excuse to himself for coming out of his way. He hastened to his new home, the house of Mr. Pete Jones, the same who believed in the inseparableness of "lickin' and larnin'."

"You're a purty gal, a'n't you? You're a purty gal, a'n't

ou? *You* air! Yes, you *air!!*" and Mrs. Means seemed so
npressed with Hannah's prettiness that she choked on
, and could get no farther. "A purty gal! you! Yes! you
ir a mighty purty gal!" and the old woman's voice rose
ll it could have been heard half a mile. "To be a santerin'
long the big road after ten o'clock with the master! Who
nows whether he's a fit man fer anybody to go with?
rter all I've been gone and done fer you! That's the way
ou pay me! Disgrace me! Yes, I say, disgrace me! You're
mean, deceitful thing. Stuck up bekase you spelt the
aster down. Ketch *me* lettin' you go to spellin'-school
-morry night! Ketch ME! Yes, ketch ME, I say!"

"Looky here, marm," said Bud, "it seems to me you're a
akin' a blamed furss about nothin'. Don't yell so's they'll
ear you three or four mile. You'll have everybody 'tween
ere and Clifty waked up." For Mrs. Means had become
excited over the idea of being caught allowing Hannah
go to spelling-school that she had raised her last
Ketch me!" to a perfect whoop. "That's the way I'm
eated," whimpered the old woman, who knew how to
ke the "injured-innocence" dodge as well as anybody.
That's the way I'm treated. You allers take sides with that
r hussy agin your own flesh and blood. You don't keer how
uch trouble I have. Not you. Not a dog-on'd bit. I may
e disgraced by that air ongrateful critter, and you set
ght here in my own house and sass me about it. A purty
llow you air! An' me a delvin' and a drudgin' fer you
l my born days. A purty son, a'n't you?"

Bud did not say another word. He sat in the chimney-
orner and whistled "Dandy Jim from Caroline." His
iversion had produced the effect he sought. For while
s tender-hearted mother poured her broadside into his
on-clad feelings, Hannah had slipped up the stairs to
er garret bed-room, and when Mrs. Means turned from

39

the callous Bud to finish her assault upon the sensitive girl, she could only gnash her teeth in disappointment

Stung by the insults to which she could not grow insensible, Hannah lay awake until the memory of that walk through the darkness came into her soul like a benediction. The harsh voice of the orge died out, and the gentle and courteous voice of Hartsook filled her soul. She recalled piece by piece the whole conversation—all the commonplace remarks about the weather; all the insignificant remarks about the crops; all the unimportant words about the spelling-school. Not for the sake of the remarks. Not for the sake of the weather. Not for the sake of the crops. Not for the sake of the spelling-school. But for the sake of the undertone. And then she traveled back over the three years of her bondage and forward over the three years to come, and fed her heart on the dim hope of rebuilding in some form the home that had been so happy. And she prayed, with more faith than ever before, for deliverance. For love brings faith. Somewhere on in the sleepless night she stood at the window. The moon was shining now, and there was the path through the pasture, and there was the fence, and there was the box-alder.

She sat there a long time. Then she saw some one come over the fence and walk to the tree, and then on toward Pete Jones's. Who could it be? She thought she recognized the figure. But she was chilled and shivering, and she crept back again into bed, and dreamed, not of the uncertain days to come, but of the blessed days that were past—of a father and a mother and a brother in a happy home. But somehow the school-master was there too.

VI

A Night at Pete Jones's

When Ralph got to Pete Jones's he found that sinister-looking individual in the act of kicking one of his many dogs out of the house.

"Come in, stranger, come in. You'll find this 'ere house full of brats, but I guess you kin kick your way around 'mong 'em. Take a cheer. Here, git out! go to thunder with you!" And with these mild imperatives he boxed one of his boys over in one direction and one of his girls over in the other. "I believe in trainin' up children to mind when they're spoke to," he said to Ralph apologetically. But it seemed to the teacher that he wanted them to mind just a little before they were spoken to.

"P'raps you'd like bed. Well, jest climb up the ladder on the outside of the house. Takes up a thunderin' sight of room to have a stairs inside, and we ha'n't got no room to spare. You'll find a bed in the furdest corner. My Pete's already got half of it, and you can take t'other half. Ef Pete goes to takin' his half in the middle, and tryin' to make you take yourn on both sides, jest kick him."

In this comfortless bed "in the furdest corner," Ralph found sleep out of the question. Pete took three fourths of the bed, and Hannah took all of his thoughts. So he lay, and looked out through the cracks in the "clapboards" (as they call rough shingles in the old West) at the stars. For the clouds had now broken away. And he lay thus recounting to himself, as a miser counts the pieces that

41

compose his hoard, every step of that road from the time he had overtaken Hannah in the hollow to the fence. Then he imagined again the pleasure of helping her over, and then he retraced the ground to the box-elder tree at the spring, and repeated to himself the conversation until he came to the part in which she said that only time and God could help her. What did she mean? What was the hidden part of her life? What was the connection between her and Shocky?

Hours wore on, and still the mind of Ralph Hartsook went back and traveled the same road, over the fence, past the box-elder, up to the inexplicable part of the conversation, and stood bewildered with the same puzzling questions about the bound girl's life.

At last he got up, drew on his clothes, and sat down on the top of the ladder, looking down over the blue-grass pasture which lay on the border between the land of Jones and the land of Means. The earth was white with moonlight. He could not sleep. Why not walk? It might enable him to sleep. And once determined on walking, he did not hesitate a moment as to the direction in which he should walk. The blue-grass pasture (was it not like unto the garden of Eden?) lay right before him. That box-elder (was it not a tree of life?) stood just in sight. To spring over the fence and take the path down the hill and over the brook was as quickly done as decided upon. To stand again under the box-elder, to climb again over the farther fence, and to walk down the road toward the school-house, was so easy and so delightful that it was done without thought. For Ralph was a man full of *élan*, who, when he saw no wrong in anything that proposed itself, was apt to follow his impulse without deliberation. And this keeping company with the stars, and the memory of a delightful walk, were so much better than the com-

42

nonplace Flat Creek life, that he threw himself into his night excursion with enthusiasm.

At last he stood in the little hollow where first he had joined himself to Hannah. It was the very spot at which Shocky, too, had met him a few mornings before. He leaned against the fence and tried again to solve the puzzle of Hannah's troubles. For that she had troubles he did not doubt. Neither did he doubt that he could help her if he could discover what they were. But he had no clue. All at once his heart stood still. He heard the thud of horses' hoofs coming down the road. Until that moment he had not felt his own loneliness. He shrank back further into the fence-corner. The horsemen were galloping. There were three of them, and there was one figure that seemed familiar to Ralph. But he could not tell who it was. Neither could he remember having seen the horse, which was a sorrel with a white left forefoot and a white nose. The men noticed him and reined up a little. Why he should have been startled by the presence of these men he could not tell, but an indefinable dread seized him. They galloped on, and he stood still shivering with a nervous fear. The cold seemed to have gotten into his bones. He remembered that the whole region lying on Flat Creek and Clifty Creek had the reputation of being infested with thieves, who practiced horse-stealing and house-breaking. For ever since the day when Murrell's Confederate bands were paralyzed by the death of their leader, there have still existed gangs of desperadoes in parts of Southern Indiana and Illinois, and in Iowa, Missouri, Kentucky, and the South-west. It is out of these materials that border ruffianism has grown, and the nine members of the Reno band who were hanged two or three years ago by lynch law, were remains of the bad blood that came into the West in the days of Daniel

43

Boone. Shall I not say that these bands of desperadoes still found among the "poor whitey," "dirt-eater" class are the outcroppings of the bad blood sent from England in convict-ships? And ought an old country to sow the fertile soil of a colony with such noxious seed?

Before Ralph was able to move, he heard the hoofs of another horse striking upon the hard ground in an easy pace. The rider was Dr. Small. He checked his horse in a cool way, and stood still a few seconds while he scrutinized Ralph. Then he rode on in the same easy gait as before. Ralph had a superstitious horror of Henry Small. And, shuddering with cold, he crept like a thief over the fence, past the tree, through the pasture, back to Pete Jones's, never once thinking of the eyes that looked out of the window at Means's. Climbing the ladder, he got into bed, and shook as with the ague. He tried to reason himself out of the foolish terror that possessed him, but he could not.

Half an hour later he heard a latch raised. Were the robbers breaking into the house below? He heard a soft tread upon the floor. Should he rise and give the alarm? Something restrained him. He reflected that a robber would be sure to stumble over some of the "brats." So he lay still and finally slumbered, only awakening when the place in which he slept was full of the smoke of frying grease from the room below.

At breakfast Pete Jones scowled. He was evidently angry about something. He treated Ralph with a rudeness not to be overlooked, as if he intended to bring on a quarrel. Hartsook kept cool, and wished he could drive from his mind all memory of the past night. Why should men on horseback have any significance to him? He was trying to regard things in this way, and from a general desire to keep on good terms with his host he went to the stable to offer his services in helping to feed the stock.

"Didn't want no saft-handed help!" was all he got in return for his well-meant offer. But just as he turned to leave the stable he saw what made him tremble again. There was the same sorrel horse with a white left forefoot and a white nose.

To shake off his nervousness, Ralph started to school before the time. But, plague upon plagues! Mirandy Means, who had seen him leave Pete Jones's, started just in time to join him where he came into the big road. Ralph was not in a good humor after his wakeful night, and to be thus dogged by Mirandy did not help the matter. So he found himself speaking crabbedly to the daughter of the leading trustee in spite of himself.

"Hanner's got a bad cold this mornin' from bein' out last night, and she can't come to spellin'-school to-night," began Mirandy, in her most simpering voice.

Ralph had forgotten that there was to be another spelling-school. It seemed to him an age since the orthographical conflict of the past night. This remark of Mirandy's fell upon his ear like an echo from the distant past. He had lived a lifetime since, and was not sure that he was the same man who was spelling for dear life against Jim Phillips twelve hours before. But he was sorry to hear that Hannah had a cold. It seemed to him, in his depressed state, that he was to blame for it. In fact, it seemed to him that he was to blame for a good many things. He seemed to have been committing sin in spite of himself. Broken nerves and sleepless nights often result in a morbid conscience. And what business had he to wander over this very road at two o'clock in the morning, and to see three galloping horsemen, one of them on a horse with a white left forefoot and a white nose? What business had he watching Dr. Small as he went home from the bedside of a dying patient near daylight in the morning? And because he felt guilty he felt cross with Mirandy, and to her remark about Hannah he only replied that "Hannah was a smart girl."

"Yes," said Mirandy, "Bud thinks so."

"Does he?" said Ralph, pricking up his ears.

"I should say so. What's him and her been a-courtin fer for a year ef he didn't think she was smart? Marm don't like it; but ef Bud and her does, and they seem to I don't see as it's marm's lookout."

When one is wretched, there is a pleasure in being entirely wretched. Ralph felt that he must have committed some unknown crime, and that some Nemesis was following him. Was Hannah deceitful? At least, if she were not, he felt sure that he could supplant Bud. But what right had he to supplant Bud?

"Did you hear the news?" cried Shocky, running out to meet him. "The Dutchman's house was robbed last night."

Ralph thought of the three men on horseback, and to save his life he could not help associating Dr. Small with them. And then he remembered the sorrel horse with the left forefoot and muzzle white, and he recalled the sound he had heard as of the lifting of a latch. And it really seemed to him that in knowing what he did he was in some sense guilty of the robbery.

VII

Ominous Remarks of Mr. Jones

The school-master's mind was like ancient Gaul—divided into three parts. With one part he mechanically performed his school duties. With another he asked himself, What shall I do about the robbery? And with the third he debated about Bud and Hannah. For Bud was not present, and it was clear that he was angry, and there was a storm brewing. In fact, is seemed to Ralph that there was storm brewing all round the sky. For Pete Jones was evidently angry at thought of having been watched, and it was fair to suppose that Dr. Small was not in any better humor than usual. And so, between Bud's jealousy and revenge and the suspicion and resentment of the men engaged in the robbery at "the Dutchman's" (as the only German in the whole region was called), Ralph's excited nerves had cause for tremor. At one moment he would resolve to have Hannah at all costs. In the next his conscience would question the rightfulness of the conclusion. Then he would make up his mind to tell all that he knew about the robbery. But if he told suspicions about Small, nobody would believe him. And if he told about Pete Jones, he really could tell only enough to bring vengeance upon himself. And how could he explain his own walk through the pasture and down the road? What business had he being out of bed at two o'clock in the morning? The circumstantial evidence was quite as strong against him as against the man on the horse with the white left forefoot and the white nose Suspicion might fasten on himself. And then what woul be the effect on his prospects? On the people at Lewi burg? On Hannah? It is astonishing how much instructio and comfort there is in a bull-dog. This slender schoo master, who had been all his life repressing the anima and developing the finer nature, now found a need o just what the bull-dog had. And so, with the thought o how his friend the dog would fight in a desperate strai he determined to take hold of his difficulties as Bull too hold of the raccoon. Moral questions he postponed fo careful decision. But for the present he set his teeth to gether in a desperate, bull-dog fashion, and he set his fee down slowly, positively, bull-doggedly. After a wretche supper at Pete Jones's he found himself at the spelling school, which, owing to the absence of Hannah and th excitement about the burglary, was a dull affair. Half th evening was spent in talking in little knots. Pete Jones ha taken the afflicted "Dutchman" under his own particula supervision.

"I s'pose," said Pete, "that them air fellers what robbe your house must a come down from Jinkins Run. They'r the blamedest set up there I ever see."

"Ya-as," said Schroeder," put how did Yinkins velle know dat I sell te medder to te Shquire, hey? How ti Yinkins know anyting 'bout the Shquire's bayin' me dre huntert in te hard gash—hey?"

"Some scoundrels down in these ere parts is a-layi in with Jinkins Run, I'll bet a hoss," said Pete. Ralp wondered whether he'd bet the one with the white le forefoot and the white nose. "Now," said Pete, "ef I coul find the feller that's a helpin' them scoundrels rob v folks, I'd help stretch him to the neardest tree."

48

"So vood I," said Schroeder. "I'd stretch him dill he baid me my dree huntert tollars pack, so I vood."

And Betsey Short, who had found the whole affair very funny, was transported with a fit of tittering at poor Schroeder's English. Ralph, fearing that his silence would excite suspicion, tried to talk. But he could not tell what he knew, and all that he said sounded so hollow and hypocritical that it made him feel guilty. And so he shut his mouth, and meditated profitably on the subject of bull-dogs. And when later he overheard the garrulous Jones declare that he'd bet a hoss he could p'int out somebody as know'd a blamed sight more'n they keer'd to tell, he made up his mind that if it came to p'inting out he should try to be even with Jones.

VIII

The Struggle in the Dark

It was a long, lonesome, fearful night that the school-master passed, lying with nerves on edge and eyes wide open in that comfortless bed in the "furdest corner" of the loft of Pete Jones's house, shivering with cold, while the light snow that was falling sifted in upon the ragged patch-work quilt that covered him. Nerves shattered by sleeplessness imagine many things, and for the first hour Ralph felt sure that Pete would cut his throat before morning. And you, friend Callow, who have blunted your palate by swallowing the Cayenne pepper of the penny-dreadfuls, or of a certain sort of Sunday-school books, you wish me to make this night exciting by a hand-to-hand contest between Ralph and a robber. You would like it better if there were a trap-door. There's nothing so convenient as a trap-door, unless it be a subterranean passage. And you'd like something of that sort just here. It's so pleasant to have one's hair stand on end, you know, when one is safe from danger to one's self. But if you want each individual hair to bristle with such a "Struggle in the Dark," you can buy trap-doors and subterranean passages dirt-cheap at the next news-stand. But it was, indeed, a real and terrible "Struggle in the Dark" that Ralph fought out at Pete Jones's.

When he had vanquished his fears of personal violence by reminding himself that it would be folly for Jones to commit murder in his own house, the question of Bud and Hannah took the uppermost place in his thoughts.

And as the image of Hannah spelling against the master came up to him, as the memory of the walk, the talk, the box-alder tree, and all the rest took possession of him, it seemed to Ralph that his very life depended upon his securing her love. He would shut his teeth like the jaws of a bull-dog, and all Bud's muscles should not prevail over his resolution and his stratagems.

It was easy to persuade himself that this was right. Hannah ought not to throw herself away on Bud Means. Men of some culture always play their conceit off against their consciences. To a man of literary habits it always seems to be a great boon that he confers on a woman when he gives her his love. Reasoning thus, Ralph had fixed his resolution, and if the night had been shorter, or sleep possible, the color of his life might have been changed.

But sometime along in the tedious hours came the memory of his childhood, the words of his mother, the old Bible stories, the aspiration after nobility of spirit, the solemn resolutions to be true to his conscience. These angels of the memory came flocking back before the animal, the bull-doggedness, had "set," as workers in plaster say. He remembered the story of David and Nathan, and it seemed to him that he, with all his abilities and ambitions and prospects, was about to rob Bud of the one ewe-lamb, the only thing he had to rejoice in his life. In getting Hannah, he would make himself unworthy of Hannah. And then there came to him a vision of the supreme value of a true character; how it was better than success, better than to be loved, better than heaven. And how near he had been to missing it! And how certain he was, when these thoughts should fade, to miss it! He was as one fighting for a great prize who feels his strength failing and is sure of defeat.

This was the real, awful "Struggle in the Dark." A human soul fighting with heaven in sight, but certain of slipping inevitably into hell! It was the same old battle. The Image of God fought with the Image of the Devil. It was the same fight that Paul described so dramatically when he represented the Spirit as contending with the Flesh. Paul also called this dreadful something the Old Adam, and I suppose Darwin would call it the remains of the Wild Beast. But call it what you will, it is the battle that every well-endowed soul must fight at some point. And to Ralph it seemed that the final victory of the Evil, the Old Adam, the Flesh, the Wild Beast, the Devil, was certain. For, was not the pure, unconscious face of Hannah on the Devil's side? And so the battle had just as well be given up at once, for it must be lost in the end.

But to Ralph, lying there in the still darkness, with his conscience as wide-awake as if it were the Day of Doom, there seemed something so terrible in this overthrow of the better nature which he knew to be inevitable as soon as the voice of conscience became blunted, that he looked about for help. He did not at first think of God; but there came into his thoughts the memory of a travel-worn Galilean peasant, hungry, sleepy, weary, tempted, tried, like other men, but having a strange, divine Victory in him by which everything evil was vanquished at his coming. He remembered how He had reached out a Hand to every helpless one, how he was the Helper of every weak one. And out of the depths of his soul he cried to the Helper, and found comfort. Not victory, but, what is better, strength. And so, without a thought of the niceties of theological distinctions, without dreaming that it was the beginning of a religious experience, he found what he needed, help. And the Helper gave his beloved sleep.

IX

Has God Forgotten Shocky?

"Pap wants to know ef you would spend tomorry and Sunday at our house?" said one of Squire Hawkins's girls, on the very next evening, which was Friday. The old Squire was thoughtful enough to remember that Ralph would not find it very pleasant "boarding out" all the time he was entitled to spend at Pete Jones's. For in view of the fact that Mr. Pete Jones sent seven children to the school, the "Master" in Flat Creek district was bound to spend two weeks in that comfortable place, sleeping in a pre-occupied bed, in the "furdest corner," with insufficient cover, under an insufficient roof, and eating floating islands of salt pork fished out of oceans of hot lard. Ralph was not slow to accept the relief offered by the hospitable justice of the peace, whose principal business seemed to be the adjustment of the pieces of which he was composed. And as Shocky traveled the same road, Ralph took advantage of the opportunity to talk with him. The Master could not dismiss Hannah wholly from his mind. He would at least read the mystery of her life, if Shocky could be prevailed on to furnish the clue.

"Poor old tree!" said Shocky, pointing to a crooked and gnarled elm standing by itself in the middle of a field. For when the elm, naturally the most graceful of trees, once gets a "bad set," as ladies say, it can grow to be the most deformed. This solitary tree had not a single straight limb.

"Why do you say 'poor old tree'?" asked Ralph.

"'Cause it's lonesome. All its old friends is dead and chopped down, and there's their stumps a-standin' jes like grave-stones. It *must* be lonesome. Some folks says it don't feel, but I think it does. Everything seems to think and feel. See it nodding its head to them other trees in the woods, and a-wantin' to shake hands! But it can't move. I think that tree must a-growed in the night."

"Why Shocky?"

"'Cause it's so crooked," and Shocky laughed at his own conceit; "must a-growed when they was no light so as it could see how to grow."

And then they walked on in silence a minute. Presently Shocky began looking up into Ralph's eyes to get a smile. "I guess that tree feels just like me. Don't you?"

"Why, how do you feel?"

"Kind o' bad and lonesome, and like as if I wanted to die, you know. Felt that way ever sence they put my father into the graveyard, and sent my mother to the poor-house and Hanner to ole Miss Means's. What kind of a place is a poor-house? Is it a poorer place than Means's? I wish I was dead and one of them clouds was a carryin' me and Hanner and mother up to where father's gone, you know! I wonder if God forgets all about poor folks when their father dies and their mother gits into the poor-house? Do you think he does? Seems so to me. May be God lost track of my father when he come away from England and crossed over the sea. Don't nobody on Flat Creek keer fer God, and I guess God don't keer fer Flat Creek. But I would though, ef he'd git my mother out of the poor-house and git Hanner away from Means's, and let me kiss my mother every night, you know, and sleep on my Hanner's arm, jes like I used to afore father died, you see."

Ralph wanted to speak, but he couldn't. And so Shocky, with his eyes looking straight ahead, and as if forgetting Ralph's presence, told over the thoughts that he had often talked over to the fence-rails and the trees. "It was real good in Mr. Pearson to take me, wasn't it? Else I'd a been bound out tell I was twenty-one, may be, to some mean man like Ole Means. And I a'n't but seven. And it would take me thirteen years to git twenty-one, and I never could live with my mother again after Hanner gets done her time. 'Cause, you see, Hanner'll be through in three more year, and I'll be ten and able to work, and we'll git a little place about as big as Granny Sanders's, and——"

Ralph did not hear another word of what Shocky said that afternoon. For there, right before them, was Granny Sanders's log cabin, with its row of lofty sun-flower stalks, now dead and dry, in front, with its rain-water barrel by the side of the low door, and its ash-barrel by the fence. In this cabin lived alone the old and shriveled hag whose hideousness gave her a reputation for almost supernatural knowledge. She was at once doctress and newspaper. She collected and disseminated medicinal herbs and personal gossip. She was in every regard indispensable to the intellectual life of the neighborhood. In the matter of her medical skill we can not express an opinion, for her "yarbs" are not to be found in the pharmacopœia of science.

What took Ralph's breath was to find Dr. Small's fine, faultless horse standing at the door. What did Henry Small want to visit this old quack for?

X

The Devil of Silence

Ralph had reason to fear Small. They were natives of the same village of Lewisburg, though Small was five years the elder. Some facts in the doctor's life had come into Ralph's possession in such a way as to confirm life-long suspicion without giving him power to expose Small, who was firmly intrenched in the good graces of the people of the county-seat village of Lewisburg, where he had grown up, and of the little cross-roads village of Clifty, where his "shingle" now hung.

Small was no ordinary villain. He was a genius. Your ordinary hypocrite talks cant. Small talked nothing. He was the coolest, the steadiest, the most silent, the most promising boy ever born in Lewisburg. He made no pretensions. He set up no claims. He uttered no professions. He went right on and lived a life above reproach. Your vulgar hypocrite makes long prayers in prayer-meeting. Small did nothing of the sort. He sat still in prayer-meeting, and listened to the elders as a modest young man should. Your commonplace hypocrite boasts. Small never alluded to himself, and thus a consummate egotist got credit for modesty. It is but an indifferent trick for a hypocrite to make temperance speeches. Dr. Small did not even belong to a temperance society. But he could never be persuaded to drink even so much as a cup of tea. There was something sublime in the quiet voice with which he would say, "Cold water, if you please," to a lady tempting him with smoking coffee on a cold morning. There was no exultation, no sense of merit in the act. Everything was done in a modest and matter-of-course way beautiful to behold. And his face was a neutral tint. Neither face nor voice expressed anything. Only a keen reader of character might have asked whether all there was in that eye could live contented with this cool, austere, self-contained life; whether there would not be somewhere a volcanic eruption. But if there was any sea of molten lava beneath, the world did not discover it. Wild boys were sick of having Small held up to them as the most immaculate of men.

Ralph had failed to get two schools for which he had applied, and had attributed both failures to certain shrugs of Dr. Small. And now, when he found Small at the house of Granny Sanders, the center of intelligence as well as of ignorance for the neighborhood, he trembled. Not that Small would say anything. He never said anything. He damned people by a silence worse than words.

Granny Sanders was not a little flattered by the visit. "Why, doctor, howdy, howdy! Come in, take a cheer. I am glad to see you. I 'lowed you'd come. Old Dr. Flounder use to say he larnt lots o' things of me. But most of the doctors sence hez been kinder stuck up, you know. But I know'd you fer a man of intelligence."

Meantime, Small, by his grave silence and attention, had almost smothered the old hag with flattery without saying one single word.

"Many's the case I've cured with yarbs and things. Nigh upon twenty year ago they was a man lived over on Wild Cat Run as had a breakin'-out on his side. 'Twas the left side, jes below the waist. Doctor couldn't do nothin'. 'Twas Doctor Peacham. He never would have nothin' to do with 'ole woman's cures.' Well, the man

57

was goin' to die. Everybody seed that. And they come a driving away over here all the way from the Wild Cat. Think of that air! I never was so flustered. But as soon as I laid eyes on that air man, I says, says I, that air man, says I, has got the shingles, says I. I know'd the minute I seed it. And if they'd a gone clean around, nothing could a saved him. I says, says I, git me a black cat. So I jist killed a black cat, and let the blood run all over the swellin'. I tell you, doctor, they's nothin' like it. That man was well in a month."

"Did you use the blood warm?" asked Small, with a solemnity most edifying.

These were the only words he had uttered since he entered the cabin.

"Laws, yes; I jest let it run right out of the cat's tail onto the breakin'-out. And fer airesipelus, I don't know nothin' so good as the blood of a black hen."

"How old?" asked the doctor.

"There you showed yer science, doctor! They's no power in a pullet. The older the black hen the better. And you know the cure fer rheumatiz." And here the old woman got down a bottle of grease. "That's ile from a black dog. Ef it's rendered right, it'll knock the hind sights off of any rheumatiz you ever see. But it must be rendered in the dark of the moon. Else a black dog's ile a'n't worth no more nor a white one's."

And all this time Small was smelling of the uncorked bottle, taking a little on his finger and feeling of it, and thus feeling his way to the heart—drier than her herbs—of the old witch. And then he went round the cabin gravely, lifting each separate bunch of dried yarbs from its nail, smelling of it, and then, by making an interrogation-point of his silent face, he managed to get a lecture from her on each article in her *materia medica,* with the most marvelous stories illustrative of their virtues. When the Granny had gotten her fill of his silent flattery, he was ready to carry forward his main purpose.

There was something weird about this silent man's ability to turn the conversation as he chose to have it go. Sitting by the Granny's tea-table, nibbling corn-bread while he drank his glass of water, having declined even her sassafras, he ceased to stimulate her medical talk and opened the vein of gossip. Once started, Granny Sanders was sure to allude to the robbery. And once on the robbery the doctor's course was clear.

"I 'low somebody not fur away is in this 'ere business!"

Not by a word, nor even by a nod, but by some motion of the eyelids, perhaps, Small indicated that he agreed with her.

"Who d'ye s'pose 'tis?"

But Dr. Small was not in the habit of supposing. He moved his head in a quiet way, just the least perceptible bit, but so that the old creature understood that he could give light if he wanted to.

"I dunno anybody that's been 'bout here long as could be suspected."

Another motion of the eyelids indicated Small's agreement with this remark.

"They a'n't nobody come in here lately 'ceppin' the master."

Small looked vacantly at the wall.

"But I 'low he's allers bore a tip-top character." The doctor was too busy looking at his corn-bread to answer this remark even by a look.

"But I think these oversmart young men'll bear looking arter, *I* do."

Dr. Small raised his eyes and let them *shine* an assent. That was all.

59

"Shouldn't wonder ef our master was overly fond of gals."

Doctor looks down at his plate.

"Had plenty of sweethearts afore he walked home with Hanner Thomson t'other night, I'll bet."

Did Dr. Small shrug his shoulder? Granny thought she detected a faint motion of the sort, but she could not be sure.

"And I think as how that a feller what trifles with gals' hearts and then runs off ten miles, may be a'n't no better'n he had orter be. That's what I says, says I."

To this general remark Dr. Small assented in his invisible—shall I say *intangible?*—way.

"I allers think, may be, that some folks has found it best to leave home and go away. You can't never tell. But when people is a-bein' robbed it's well to look out. Hey?"

"I think so," said Small quietly, and, having taken his hat and bowed a solemn and respectful adieu, he departed.

He had not spoken twenty words, but he had satisfied the newsmonger of Flat Creek that Ralph was a bad character at home, and worthy of suspicion of burglary.

XI

Miss Martha Hawkins

"It's very good for the health to dig in the elements. I was quite emaciated last year at the East, and the doctor told me to dig in the elements. I got me a florial hoe and dug, and it's been most excellent for me." Time, the Saturday following the Friday on which Ralph kept Shocky company as far as the "forks" near Granny Sanders's house. Scene, the Squire's garden. Ralph helping that worthy magistrate perform sundry little jobs such as a warm winter day suggests to the farmer. Miss Martha Hawkins, the Squire's niece, and his housekeeper in his present bereaved condition, leaning over the palings—pickets she called them—of the garden fence, talking to the master. Miss Hawkins was recently from Massachusetts. How many people there are in the most cultivated communities whose education is partial!

"It's very common for school-masters to dig in the elements at the East," proceeded Miss Martha. Like many other people born in the celestial empires (of which there are three—China, Virginia, Massachusetts), Miss Martha was not averse to reminding outside barbarians of her good fortune in this regard. It did her good to speak of the East.

Now Ralph was amused with Miss Martha. She really had a good deal of intelligence despite her affectation, and conversation with her was both interesting and diverting. It helped him to forget Hannah, and Bud, and the robbery, and all the rest, and she was so delighted to find somebody to make an impression on that she had come out to talk while Ralph was at work. But just at this moment the school-master was not so much interested in her interesting remarks, nor so much amused by her amusing remarks, as he should have been. He saw a man coming down the road riding one horse and leading another, and he recognized the horses at a distance. It must be Bud who was riding Means's bay mare and leading Bud's roan colt. Bud had been to mill, and as the man who owned the horse-mill kept but one old blind horse himself, it was necessary that Bud should take two. It required three horses to run the mill; the old blind one could grind the grist, but the two others had to overcome the friction of the clumsy machine.

But it was not about the horse-mill that Ralph was thinking, nor about the two horses. Since that Wednesday evening on which he escorted Hannah home from the spelling-school he had not seen Bud Means. If he had any lingering doubts of the truth of what Mirandy had said, they had been dissipated by the absence of Bud from school.

"When I was to Bosting——" Miss Martha was *to* Boston only once in her life, but as her visit to that sacred city was the most important occurrence of her life, she did not hesitate to air her reminiscences of it frequently. "When I was to Bosting," she was just saying, when, following the indications of Ralph's eyes, she saw Bud coming up the hill near Squire Hawkins's house. Bud looked red and sulky, and to Ralph's and Miss Martha Hawkins's polite recognitions he returned only a surly nod. They both saw that he was angry. Ralph was able to guess the meaning of his wrath.

Toward evening Ralph strolled through the Squire's

cornfield toward the woods. The memory of the walk with Hannah was heavy upon the heart of the young master, and there was comfort in the very miserableness of the cornstalks with their disheveled blades hanging like tattered banners and rattling discordantly in the rising wind. Wandering without purpose, Ralph followed the rows of stalks first one way and then the other in a zigzag line, turning a right angle every minute or two. At last he came out in a woods mostly of beech, and he pleased his melancholy fancy by kicking the dry and silky leaves before him in billows, while the soughing of the wind through the long, vibrant boughs and slender twigs of the beech forest seemed to put the world into the wailing minor key of his own despair.

What a fascination there is in a path come upon suddenly without a knowledge of its termination! Here was one running in easy, irregular curves through the wood, now turning gently to the right in order to avoid a stump, now swaying suddenly to the left to gain an easier descent at a steep place, and now turning wantonly to the one side or the other, as if from very caprice in the man who by idle steps unconsciously marked the line of the foot-path at first. Ralph could not resist the impulse—who could?—to follow the path and find out its destination, and following it he came presently into a lonesome hollow, where a brook gurgled among the heaps of bare limestone rocks that filled its bed. Following the path still, he came upon a queer little cabin built of round logs, in the midst of a small garden patch inclosed by a brush fence. The stick chimney, daubed with clay and topped with a barrel open at both ends, made this a typical cabin.

It flashed upon Ralph that this place must be Rocky Hollow, and that this was the house of old John Pearson,

63

the one-legged basket-maker, and his rheumatic wife—the house that hospitably sheltered Shocky. Following his impulse, he knocked and was admitted, and was not a little surprised to find Miss Martha Hawkins there before him.

"You here, Miss Hawkins?" he said when he had returned Shocky's greeting and shaken hands with the old couple.

"Bless you, yes," said the old lady. "That blessed gyirl"—the old lady called her a girl by a sort of figure of speech perhaps—"that blessed gyirl's the kindest creetur you ever saw—comes here every day, most, to cheer a body up with somethin' or nuther."

Miss Martha blushed, and said "she came because Rocky Hollow looked so much like a place she used to know at the East. Mr. and Mrs. Pearson were the kindest people. They reminded her of people she knew at the East. When she was to Bosting——"

Here the old basket-maker lifted his head from his work, and said: "Pshaw! that talk about kyindness" (he was a Kentuckian and said *kyindness*) "is all humbug. I wonder so smart a woman as you don't know better. You come nearder to bein' kyind than anybody I know; but, laws a me! we're all selfish akordin' to my tell."

"You wasn't selfish when you set up with my father most every night for two weeks," said Shocky, as he handed the old man a splint.

"Yes, I was, too!" This in a tone that made Ralph tremble. "Your father was a miserable Britisher. I'd fit red-coats, in the war of eighteen-twelve, and lost my leg by one of 'em stickin' his dog-on'd bagonet right through it, that night at Lundy's Lane; but my messmate killed him though, which is a satisfaction to think on. And I didn't like your father, 'cause he was a Britisher. But ef

64

he'd a died right here in this free country, 'thout nobody to give him a drink of water, blamed ef I wouldn't a been ashamed to set on the platform at a Fourth-of-July barbecue, and to hold up my wooden leg for to make the boys cheer! That was the selfishest thing I ever done. We're all selfish akordin' to my tell."

"You wasn't selfish when you took me that night, you know," and Shocky's face beamed with gratitude.

"Yes, I war too, you little sass-box! What did I take you fer? Hey? Bekase I didn't like Pete Jones nor Bill Jones. They're thieves, dog on 'em!"

Ralph shivered a little. The horse with the white fore-foot and white nose galloped before his eyes again.

"They're a set of thieves. That's what they air."

"Please, Mr. Pearson, be careful. You'll get into trouble, you know, by talking that way," said Miss Hawkins. "You're just like a man that I knew at the East."

"Why, do you think an old soldier like me, hobbling on a wooden leg, is afraid of them thieves? Didn't I face the Britishers? Didn't I come home late last Wednesday night? I rather guess I must a took a little too much at Welch's grocery, and laid down in the middle of the street to rest. The boys thought 'twas funny to crate me. I woke up kind a cold, 'bout one in the mornin'. 'Bout two o'clock I come up Means's hill, and didn't I see Pete Jones, and them others what robbed the Dutchman, and somebody, I dunno who, a crossin' the blue-grass paster to*wards* Jones's?" (Ralph shivered.) "Don't shake your finger at me, old woman. Tongue is all I've got to fight with now; but I'll fight them thieves tell the sea goes dry, I will. Shocky, gimme a split."

"But you wasn't selfish when you tuck me." Shocky stuck to his point most positively.

"Yes, I was, you little tow-headed fool! I didn't take

65

you kase I was good, not a bit of it. I hated Bill Jones what keeps the poor-house, and I knowed him and Pete would get you bound to some of their click, and I didn't want no more thieves raised; so when your mother hobbled, with you a leadin' her, poor blind thing! all the way over here on that winter night, and said, 'Mr. Pearson, you're all the friend I've got, and I want you to save my boy,' why, you see I was selfish as ever I could be in takin' of you. Your mother's cryin' sot me a cryin' too. We're all selfish in everything, akordin' to my tell. Blamed ef we ha'n't, Miss Hawkins, only sometimes I'd think you was real benev'lent ef I didn't know we war all selfish."

XII

The Hardshell Preacher

"They's preachin' down to Bethel Meetin'-house to-day," said the Squire at breakfast. Twenty years in the West could not cure Squire Hawkins of saying "to" for "at." "I rather guess as how the ole man Bosaw will give per-tickeler fits to our folks to-day." For Squire Hawkins, having been expelled from the "Hardshell" church of which Mr. Bosaw was pastor, for the grave offense of joining a temperance society, had become a member of the "Reformers," the very respectable people who now call themselves "Disciples," but whom the profane will persist in calling "Campbellites." They had a church in the village of Clifty, three miles away.

I know that explanations are always abominable to story readers, as they are to story writers, but as so many of my readers have never had the inestimable privilege of sitting under the gospel as it is ministered in enlightened neighborhoods like Flat Creek, I find myself under the necessity—need-cessity the Rev. Mr. Bosaw would call it—of rising to explain. Some people think the "Hard-shells" a myth, and some sensitive Baptist people at the East resent all allusion to them. But the "Hardshell Bap-tists," or, as they are otherwise called, the "Whisky Bap-tists," and the "Forty-gallon Baptists," exist in all the old Western and South-western States. They call them-selves "Anti-means Baptists" from their Antinomian tenets. Their confession of faith is a caricature of Calvinism, and is expressed by their preachers about as follows: "Ef you're elected you'll be saved; ef you a'n't, you'll be damned. God'll take keer of his elect. It's a sin to run Sunday-schools, or temp'rince s'cieties, or to send missionaries. You let God's business alone. What is to be will be, and you can't hender it." This writer has attended a Sunday-school, the superintendent of which was solemnly arraigned and expelled from the Hardshell Church for "meddling with God's business" by holding a Sunday-school. Of course the Hardshells are prodigiously illiterate, and often vicious. Some of their preachers are notorious drunkards. They sing their sermons out sometimes for three hours at a stretch. Ralph found that he was to ride the "clay-bank mare," the only one of the horses that would "carry double," and that consequently he would have—according to Hoosier custom—to take Miss Hawkins behind him. If it had been Hannah instead, Ralph might not have objected to this "young Lochinvar" mode of riding with a lady on "the croup," but Martha Hawkins was another affair. He had only this consolation: his keeping the company of Miss Hawkins might serve to disarm the resentment of Bud. At all events, he had no choice. What designs the Squire had in this arrangement he could not tell; but at any rate the clay-bank mare carried him to meeting on that December morning, with Martha Hawkins behind. And as Miss Hawkins was not used to this mode of locomotion, she was in a state of delightful fright every time the horse sank to the knees in the soft, yellow Flat Creek clay.

"We don't go to church so at the East," she said. "The mud isn't so deep at the East. When I was to Bosting——" but Ralph never heard what happened when she was to Bosting, for just as she said Bosting the mare put her foot into a deep hole molded by the foot of the Squire's horse, and already full of muddy water. As the mare's foot went twelve inches down into this track, the muddy water spurted higher than Miss Hawkins's head, and mottled her dress with golden spots of clay. She gave a little shriek, and declared that she had never "seen it so at the East."

The journey seemed a little long to Ralph, who found that the subjects upon which he and Miss Hawkins could converse were few; but Miss Martha was determined to keep things going, and once, when the conversation had died out entirely, she made a desperate effort to renew it by remarking, as they met a man on horseback, "That horse switches his tail just as they do at the East. When I was to Bosting I saw horses switch their tails just that way."

What surprised Ralph was to see that Flat Creek went to meeting. Everybody was there—the Meanses, the Joneses, the Bantas, and all the rest. Everybody on Flat Creek seemed to be there, except the old wooden-legged basket-maker. His family was represented by Shocky, who had come, doubtless, to get a glimpse of Hannah, not to hear Mr. Bosaw preach. In fact, few were thinking of the religious service. They went to church as a common resort to hear the news, and find out what was the current sensation.

On this particular morning there seemed to be some unusual excitement. Ralph perceived it as he rode up. An excited crowd, even though it be at a church-door on Sunday morning, can not conceal its agitation. Ralph deposited Miss Hawkins on the stile, and then got down himself, and paid her the closest attention to the door. This attention was for Bud's benefit. But Bud only stood with his hands in his pockets, scowling worse than ever. Ralph did not go in at the door. It was not the Flat Creek custom. The men gossiped outside, while the women chatted within. Whatever may have been the cause of the excitement, Ralph could not get at it. When he entered a little knot of people they became embarrassed, and the group dissolved itself, and its component parts joined other companies. What had the current of conversation to do with him? He overheard Pete Jones saying that the blamed old wooden leg was in it any how. He'd been seen goin' home at two in the mornin'. And he could name somebody else ef he choosed. But it was best to clean out one at a time. And just then there was a murmur: "Meetin's took up." And the masculine element filled the empty half of the "hewed-log" church.

When Ralph saw Hannah looking utterly dejected, his heart smote him, and the great struggle set in again. Had it not been for the thought of the other battle, and the comforting presence of the Helper, I fear Bud's interests would have fared badly. But Ralph, with the spirit of a martyr, resolved to wait until he knew what the result of Bud's suit should be, and whether, indeed, the young Goliath had prior claims, as he evidently thought he had. He turned hopefully to the sermon, determined to pick up any crumbs of comfort that might fall from Mr. Bosaw's meager table.

In reporting a single specimen passage of Mr. Bosaw's sermon, I shall not take the liberty which Thucydides and other ancient historians did, of making the sermon and putting it in the hero's mouth, but shall give that which can be vouched for.

"You see, my respective hearers," he began—but alas! I can never picture to you the rich red nose, the see-sawing gestures, the nasal resonance, the sniffle, the melancholy minor key, and all that. "My respective hearers-ah, you see-ah as how-ah as my tex'-ah says that the ox-ah knoweth his owner-ah, and-ah the ass-ah his master's crib-ah. A-h-h! Now, my respective hearers-ah, they're a mighty sight of resemblance-ah atwext men-ah and oxen-ah" [Ralph could not help reflecting that there was a mighty sight of resemblance between some men and asses. But the preacher did not see this analogy. It lay too close to him], "bekase-ah, you see, men-ah is mighty like oxen-ah. For they's a tremengious defference-ah atwixt defferent oxen-ah, jest as thar is atwext defferent men-ah; fer the ox knoweth-ah his owner-ah, and the ass-ah, his master's crib-ah. Now, my respective hearers-ah" [the preacher's voice here grew mellow, and the succeeding sentences were in the most pathetic and lugubrious voice], "you all know-ah that your humble speaker-ah has got-ah jest the best yoke of steers-ah in this township-ah." [Here Betsey Short shook the floor with a suppressed titter.] "They a'n't no sech steers as them air two of mine-ah in this whole kedentry-ah. Them crack oxen over at Clifty-ah ha'n't a patchin' to mine-ah. Fer the ox knoweth his owner-ah, and the ass-ah his master's crib-ah.

"Now, my respective hearers-ah, they's a right smart sight of defference-ah atwext them air two oxen-ah, jest like they is atwext defferent men-ah. Fer-ah" [here the speaker grew earnest, and sawed the air, from this to the close, in a most frightful way], "fer-ah, you see-ah, when I go out-ah in the mornin'-ah to yoke-ah up-ah them air steers-ah, and I says-ah, 'Wo, Berry-ah! *Wo, Berry-ah!* Wo, BERRY-AH!' why Berry-ah jest stands stock still-ah and don't hardly breathe-ah while I put on the yoke-ah, and put in the bow-ah, and put in the key-ah, fer, my brethering-ah and sistering-ah, the ox knoweth his owner-ah, and the ass-ah his master's crib-ah. Hal-le-lu-ger-ah!

71

"But-ah, my hearers-ah, but-ah when I stand at t'other eend of the yoke-ah, and say, 'Come, Buck-ah! *Come, Buck-ah!* Come, Buck-ah! COME, BUCK-AH!' why what do you think-ah? Buck-ah, that ornery ole Buck-ah, 'stid of comin' right along-ah and puttin' his neck under-ah, acts jest like some men-ah what is fools-ah. Buck-ah jest kinder sorter stands off-ah, and kinder sorter puts his head down-ah this ere way-ah, and kinder looks mad-ah, and says, Boo-*oo*-oo-OO-*ah!*"

Alas! Hartsook found no spiritual edification there, and he was in no mood to be amused. And so, while the sermon drew on through two dreary hours, he forgot the preacher in noticing a bright green lizard which, having taken up its winter quarters behind the tin candlestick that hung just back of the preacher's head, had been deceived by the genial warmth coming from the great box-stove, and now ran out two or three feet from his shelter, looking down upon the red-nosed preacher in a most confidential and amusing manner. Sometimes he would retreat behind the candlestick, which was not twelve inches from the preacher's head, and then rush out again. At each reappearance Betsey Short would stuff her handkerchief into her mouth and shake in a most distressing way. Shocky wondered what the lizard was winking at the preacher about. And Miss Martha thought that it reminded her of a lizard that she see at the East, the time she was to Bosting, in a jar of alcohol in the Natural History Rooms.

The Squire was not disappointed in his anticipation that Mr. Bosaw would attack his denomination with some fury. In fact, the old preacher outdid himself in his violent indignation at "these people that follow Campbell-ah, that thinks-ah that obejience-ah will save 'em-ah, and that belongs-ah to temp'rince societies-ah and Sunday-

chools-ah, and them air things-ah, that's not ortherized
n the Bible-ah, but comes of the devil-ah, and takes folks
s belongs to 'em to hell-ah."

As they came out the door Ralph rallied enough to
emark: "He did attack your people, Squire."

"Oh! yes," said the Squire. "Didn't you see the Sarpent
nspirin' him?"

But when the long, long hours were ended Ralph got
n the clay-bank mare and rode up alongside the stile
vhence Miss Martha mounted. And as he went away
vith a heavy heart, he overheard Pete Jones call out to
omebody:

"We'll tend to his case a Christmas." Christmas was two
lays off.

And Miss Martha remarked with much trepidation that
·oor Pearson would have to leave. She'd always been
fraid that would be the end of it. It reminded her of
omething she heard at the East the time she was down
o Bosting.

XIII

A Struggle for the Mastery

The school closed on Monday evening as usual. The boys had been talking in knots all day. Nothing but the bull-dog in the slender, resolute young master had kept down the rising storm. Let a teacher lose moral support at home, and he can not long govern a school. Ralph had effectually lost his popularity in the district, and the worst of it was that he could not divine from just what quarter the ill wind came, except that he felt sure of Small's agency in it somewhere. Even Hannah had slighted him, when he called at Means's on Monday morning to draw the pittance of pay that was due him.

He had expected a petition for a holiday on Christmas day. Such holidays are deducted from the teacher's time, and it is customary for the boys to "turn out" the teacher who refuses to grant them, by barring him out of the school-house on Christmas and New Year's morning. Ralph had intended to grant a holiday if it should be asked, but it was not asked. Hank Banta was the ring-leader in the disaffection, and he had managed to draw the surly Bud, who was present this morning, into it. It is but fair to say that Bud was in favor of making a request before resorting to extreme measures, but he was overruled. He gave it as his solemn opinion that the master was mighty peart, and they would be beat any how some way, but he would lick the master fer two cents ef he warn't so slim that he'd feel like he was fighting a baby.

And all that day things looked black. Ralph's countenance was cold and hard as stone, and Shocky trembled where he sat in front of him. Betsey Short tittered rather more than usual. A riot or a murder would have seemed amusing to her.

School was dismissed, and Ralph, instead of returning to the Squire's, set out for the village of Clifty a few miles away. No one knew what he went for, and some suggested that he had "sloped." But Bud said "he warn't that air kind. He was one of them air sort as died in ther tracks, was Mr. Hartsook. They'd find him on the ground nex' morning, and he 'lowed the master war made of that air sort of stuff as would burn the dog-on'd ole school-house to ashes, or blow it into splinters, but what he'd beat. Howsumdever he'd said he was a-goin' to help, and help he would; but all the sinnoo in Golier wouldn' be no account agin the cute they was in the head of the master."

But Bud, discouraged as he was with the fear of Ralph's "cute," went like a martyr to the stake and took his place with the rest in the school-house at nine o'clock at night. It may have been Ralph's intention to have pre-occupied the school-house, for at ten o'clock Hank Banta was set shaking from head to foot at seeing a face that looked like the master's at the window. He waked up Bud and told him about it.

"Well, what are you a-tremblin' about, you coward?" growled Bud. "He won't shoot you; but he'll beat you at his game, I'll bet a hoss, and me, too, and make us both as 'shamed of ourselves as dogs with tin-kittles to their tails. You don't know the master, though he did duck you. But he'll larn you a good lesson this time, and me too, like as not." And Bud soon snored again, but Hank shook with fear every time he looked at the blackness outside the windows. He was sure he heard foot-falls. He would have given anything to have been at home.

When morning came, the pupils began to gather early. A few boys who were likely to prove of service in the coming siege were admitted through the window, and then everything was made fast, and a "snack" was eaten.

"How do you 'low he'll git in?" said Hank, trying to hide his fear.

"How do I 'low?" said Bud. "I don't 'low nothin' about it. You might as well ax me where I 'low the nex' shootin' star is a-goin' to drap. Mr. Hartsook's mighty onsartin. But he'll git in, though, and tan your hide fer you, you see ef he don't. *Ef* he don't blow up the school-house with gun-powder!" This last was thrown in by way of alleviating the fears of the cowardly Hank, for whom Bud had a great contempt.

The time for school had almost come. The boys inside were demoralized by waiting. They began to hope that the master had "sloped." They dreaded to see him coming.

"I don't believe he'll come," said Hank, with a cold shiver. "It's past school-time."

"Yes, he will come, too," said Bud. "And he 'lows to come in here mighty quick. I don't know how. But he'll be a-standin' at that air desk when it's nine o'clock. I'll bet a thousand dollars on that. *Ef* he don't take it into his head to blow us up!" Hank was now white.

Some of the parents came along, accidentally of course, and stopped to see the fun, sure that Bud would thrash the master if he tried to break in. Small, on the way to see a patient perhaps, reined up in front of the door. Still no Ralph. It was just five minutes before nine. A rumor now gained currency that he had been seen going to Clifty the evening before, and that he had not come back, though in fact Ralph had come back, and had slept at Squire Hawkins's.

"There's the master," cried Betsey Short, who stood out in the road, shivering and giggling alternately. For Ralph at that moment emerged from the sugar-camp by the school-house, carrying a board.

"Ho! ho!" laughed Hank, "he thinks he'll smoke us out. I guess he'll find us ready." The boys had let the fire burn down, and there was now nothing but hot hickory coals on the hearth.

"I tell you he'll come in. He didn't go to Clifty fer nothin'," said Bud, who sat still on one of the benches which leaned against the door. "I don't know how, but they's lots of ways of killing a cat besides chokin' her with butter. He'll come in—*ef* he don't blow us all sky-high!"

Ralph's voice was now heard, demanding that the door be opened.

"Let's open her," said Hank, turning livid with fear at the firm, confident tone of the master.

Bud straightened himself up. "Hank, you're a coward. I've got a mind to kick you. You got me into this blamed mess, and now you want to flunk. You jest tech one of these ere fastenings, and I'll lay you out flat of your back afore you can say Jack Robinson."

The teacher was climbing to the roof with the board in hand.

"That air won't win," laughed Pete Jones outside. He saw that there was no smoke. Even Bud began to hope that Ralph would fail for once. The master was now on the ridge-pole of the school-house. He took a paper from his pocket, and deliberately poured the contents down the chimney.

Mr. Pete Jones shouted "Gunpowder!" and started down the road to be out of the way of the explosion. Dr. Small remembered, probably, that his patient might die while he sat there, and started on.

But Ralph emptied the paper, and laid the board over the chimney. What a row there was inside! The benches that were braced against the door were thrown down, and Hank Banta rushed out, rubbing his eyes, coughing frantically, and sure that he had been blown up. All the rest followed, Bud bringing up the rear sulkily, but coughing and sneezing for dear life. Such a smell of sulphur as came from that school-house!

Betsey had to lean against the fence to giggle.

As soon as all were out, Ralph threw the board off the chimney, leaped to the ground, entered the school-house, and opened the windows. The school soon followed him, and all was still.

"Would he thrash?" This was the important question in Hank Banta's mind. And the rest looked for a battle with Bud.

"It is just nine o'clock," said Ralph, consulting his watch, "and I'm glad to see you all here promptly. I should have given you a holiday if you had asked me like gentlemen yesterday. On the whole, I think I shall give you a holiday, any how. The school is dismissed."

And Hank felt foolish.

And Bud secretly resolved to thrash Hank or the master, he didn't care which.

And Mirandy looked the love she could not utter.

And Betsey giggled.

XIV

A Crisis with Bud

Ralph sat still at his desk. The school had gone. All at once he became conscious that Shocky sat yet in his accustomed place upon the hard, backless bench.

"Why, Shocky, haven't you gone yet?"

"No—sir—I was waitin' to see if you warn't a goin', too—I—"

"Well?"

"I thought it would make me feel as if God warn't quite so fur away to talk to you. It did the other day."

The master rose and put his hand on Shocky's head. Was it the brotherhood in affliction that made Shocky's words choke him so? Or, was it the weird thoughts that he expressed? Or, was it the recollection that Shocky was Hannah's brother? Hannah—so far, far away from him now! At any rate, Shocky, looking up for the smile on which he fed, saw the relaxing of the master's face, that had been as hard as stone, and felt just one hot tear on his hand.

"P'r'aps God's forgot you, too," said Shocky in a sort of half-soliloquy. "Better get away from Flat Creek. You see God forgets everybody down here. 'Cause 'most everybody forgets God, 'cept Mr. Bosaw, and I 'low God don't no ways keer to be remembered by sich as him. Leastways I wouldn't if I was God, you know. I wonder what becomes of folks when God forgets 'em?" And Shocky, seeing that the master had resumed his seat and was looking absently into the fire, moved slowly out the door.

"Shocky!" called the master.

The little poet came back and stood before him.

"Shocky, you mustn't think God has forgotten you. God brings things out right at last." But Ralph's own faith was weak, and his words sounded hollow and hypocritical to himself. Would God indeed bring things out right?

He sat musing a good while, trying to convince himself of the truth of what he had just been saying to Shocky—that God would indeed bring things out right at last. Would it all come out right if Bud married Hannah? Would it all come out right if he were driven from Flat Creek with a dark suspicion upon his character? Did God concern himself with these things? Was there any God? It was the same old struggle between Doubt and Faith. And when Ralph looked up, Shocky had departed.

In the next hour Ralph fought the old battle of Armageddon. I shall not describe it. You will fight it in your own way. No two alike. The important thing is the End. If you come out as he did, with the doubt gone and the trust in God victorious, it matters little just what shape the battle may take. Since Jacob became Israel there have never been two such struggles alike, save in that they all end either in victory or defeat.

It was after twelve o'clock on that Christmas day when Ralph put his head out the door of the school-house and called out: "Bud, I'd like to see you."

Bud did not care to see the master, for he had inly resolved to "thrash him" and have done with him. But he couldn't back out, certainly not in sight of the others who were passing along the road with him.

"I don't want the rest of you," said Ralph in a decided way, as he saw that Hank and one or two others were resolved to come also.

"Thought may be you'd want somebody to see far play," said Hank as he went off sheepishly.

"If I did, you would be the last one I should ask," said Ralph. "There's no unfair play in Bud, and there is in you." And he shut the door.

"Now, looky here, Mr. Ralph Hartsook," said Bud. "You don't come no gum games over me with your saft sodder and all that. I've made up my mind. You've got to promise to leave these ere diggins, or I've got to thrash you."

"You'll have to thrash me, then," said Ralph, turning a little pale, but remembering the bull-dog. "But you'll tell me what it's all about, won't you?"

"You know well enough. Folks says you know more bout the robbery at the Dutchman's than you orter. But I don't believe them. Fer them as says it is liars and thieves theirselves. 'Ta'n't fer none of that. And I shan't tell you what it *is* fer. So now, if you won't travel, why, take off your coat and git ready fer a thrashing."

The master took off his coat and showed his slender arms. Bud laid his off, and showed the physique of a prize-fighter.

"You a'n't a-goin' to fight *me?*" said Bud.

"Not unless you make me."

"Why I could chaw you all up."

"I know that."

"Well, you're the grittiest feller I ever did see, and ef you'd jest kep off of my ground I wouldn't a-touched you. But I a'n't agoin' to be cut out by no feller a livin' thout thrashin' him in an inch of his life. You see I wanted to git out of this Flat Crick way. We're a low-lived set here in Flat Crick. And I says to myself, I'll try to be somethin' more nor Pete Jones, and dad, and these other triflin', good-fer-northin' ones 'bout here. And when you

81

come I says, There's one as'll help me. And what do you do with your book-larnin' and town manners but start right out to git away the gal that I'd picked out, when I'd picked her out kase I thought, not bein' Flat Crick born herself, she might help a feller to do better! Now I won't let nobody cut me out without givin' 'em the best thrashin' it's in these 'ere arms to give."

"But I haven't tried to cut you out."

"You can't fool *me*."

"Bud, listen to me, and then thrash me if you will. I went with that girl once. When I found you had some claims, I gave her up. Not because I was afraid of you, for I would rather have taken the worst thrashing you can give me than give her up. But I haven't spoken to her since the night of the first spelling-school."

"You lie!" said Bud, doubling his fists.

Ralph grew red.

"You was a-waitin' on her last Sunday right afore my eyes, and a-tryin' to ketch my attention too. So when you're ready, say so."

"Bud, there is some misunderstanding." Hartsook spoke slowly and felt bewildered. "I tell you that I did not speak to Hannah last Sunday, and you know I didn't."

"Hanner!" Bud's eyes grew large. "Hanner!" Here he gasped for breath, and looked around. "Hanner!" He couldn't get any further than the name at first. "Why, plague take it, who said Hanner?"

"Mirandy said you were courting Hannah," said Ralph, feeling round in a vague way to get his ideas together.

"Mirandy! Thunder! You believed Mirandy! Well! Now looky here, Mr. Hartsook, ef you was to say that my sister lied, I'd lick you till yer hide wouldn' hold shucks. But *I* say, atwixt you and me and the gate-post, don't you never believe nothing that Mirandy Means says. Her and marm has set theirselves like fools to git you. Hanner! Well, she's a mighty nice gal, but you're welcome to her. I never tuck no shine that air way. But I was out of school last Thursday and Friday a shucking corn to take to mill a Saturday. And when I come past the Squire's and seed you talking to a gal as is a gal, you know"—here Bud hesitated and looked foolish—"I felt hoppin' mad."

Bud put on his coat.

Ralph put on his coat.

Then they shook hands and Bud went out. Ralph sat looking into the fire. There was no conscientious difficulty now in the way of his claiming Hannah. The dry fore-stick lying on the rude stone andirons burst into a blaze. The smoldering hope in the heart of Ralph Hartsook did the same. He could have Hannah if he could win her. But there came slowly back the recollection of his lost standing in Flat Creek. There was circumstantial evidence against him. It was evident that Hannah believed something of this. What other stories Small may have put in circulation he did not know. Would Small try to win Hannah's love, to throw it away again, as he had done with others? At least he would not spare any pains to turn the heart of the bound girl against Ralph.

The bright flame on the forestick which Ralph had been watching flickered and burned low.

XV

The Church of the Best Licks

Just as the flame on the forestick, which Ralph had
watched so intensely, flickered and burned low, and just
as Ralph with a heavy but not quite hopeless heart rose
to leave, the latch lifted and Bud re-entered.

"I wanted to say something," he stammered, "but
you know it's hard to say it. I ha'n't no book-larnin' to
speak of, and some things is hard to say when a man
ha'n't got book-words to say 'em with. And they's some
things a man can't hardly ever say any how to anybody."

Here Bud stopped. But Ralph spoke in such a matter-
of-course way in reply that he felt encouraged to go on.

"You gin up Hanner kase you thought she belonged to
me. That's more'n I'd done by a long shot. Now, arter
I left here jest now, I says to myself, a man what can
gin up his gal on account of sech a feeling fer the rights
of a Flat Cricker like me, why, dog on it, says I, sech a
man is the man as can help me do better. I don't know
whether you're a Hardshell or a Saftshell, or a Methodist,
or a Campbellite, or a New Light, or a United Brother,
or a Millerite, or what not. But I says, the man what can
do the clean thing by a ugly feller like me and stick to
it, when I was jest ready to eat him up, is a kind of a
man to tie to."

Here Bud stopped in fright at his own volubility, for
he had run his words off like a piece learned by heart, as

84

though afraid that if he stopped he would not have courage to go on.

Ralph said that he did not yet belong to any church,
and he was afraid he couldn't do Bud much good. But
his tone was full of sympathy, and, what is better than
sympathy, a yearning for sympathy.

"You see," said Bud, "I wanted to git out of this low-
lived, Flat Crick way of livin'. We're a hard set down
here, Mr. Hartsook. And I'm gittin' to be one of the
hardest of 'em. But I never could git no good out of
Bosaw with his whisky and meanness. And I went to the
Mount Tabor church oncet. I heard a man discussin' bap-
tism, and regeneration, and so on. That didn't seem no
cure for me. I went to a revival over at Clifty. Well,
'twarnt no use. First night they was a man that spoke
about Jesus Christ in sech a way that I wanted to foller
him everywhere. But I didn't feel fit. Next night I come
back with my mind made up that I'd try Jesus Christ, and
see ef he'd have me. But laws! they was a big man that
night that preached hell. Not that I don't believe they's
a hell. They's plenty not a thousand miles away as de-
serves it, and I don't know as I'm too good for it myself.
But he pitched it at us, and stuck it in our faces in sech
a way that I got mad. And I says, Well, ef God sends
me to hell he can't make me holler 'nough no how. You
see my dander was up. And when my dander's up, I
wouldn't gin up fer the devil hisself. The preacher was so
insultin' with his way of doin' it. He seemed to be kind
of glad that we was to be damned, and he preached
somethin' like some folks swears. It didn't sound a bit
like the Christ the little man preached about the night
afore. So what does me and a lot of fellers do but slip
out and cut off the big preacher's stirrups, and hang them

85

on to the rider of the fence, and then set his hoss loose! And from that day, sometimes I did, and sometimes I didn't, want to be better. And to-day it seemed to me that you must know somethin' as would help me."

Nothing is worse than a religious experience kept ready to be exposed to the gaze of everybody, whether the time is appropriate or not. But never was a religious experience more appropriate than the account which Ralph gave to Bud of his Struggle in the Dark. The confession of his weakness and wicked selfishness was a great comfort to Bud.

"Do you think that Jesus Christ would—would—well, do you think he'd help a poor, unlarnt Flat Cricker like me?"

"I think he was a sort of a Flat Creeker himself," said Ralph, slowly and very earnestly.

"You don't say?" said Bud, almost getting off his seat.

"Why, you see the town he lived in was a rough place. It was called Nazareth, which meant 'Bushtown.' "

"You don't say?"

"And he was called a Nazarene, which was about the same as 'backwoodsman.' "

And Ralph read the different passages which he had studied at Sunday-school, illustrating the condescension of Jesus, the stories of the publicans, the harlots, the poor, who came to him. And he read about Nathanael, who lived only six miles away, saying "Can any good thing come out of Nazareth?"

"Just what Clifty folks says about Flat Crick," broke in Bud.

"Do you think I could begin without being baptized?" he added presently.

"Why not? Let's begin now to do the best we can, by his help."

86

"You mean, then, that I'm to begin now to put in my best licks for Jesus Christ, and that he'll help me?"

This shocked Ralph's veneration a little. But it was the sincere utterance of an earnest soul. It may not have been an orthodox start, but it was the one start for Bud. And there be those who have repeated with the finest æsthetic appreciation the old English liturgies who have never known religious aspiration so sincere as that of this ignorant young Hercules, whose best confession was that he meant hereafter "to put in his best licks for Jesus Christ." And there be those who can define repentance and faith to the turning of a hair who never made so genuine a start for the kingdom of heaven as Bud Means did.

Ralph said yes, that he thought that was just it. At least, he guessed if there was something more, the man that was putting in his best licks would be sure to find it out.

"Do you think he'd help a feller? Seems to me it would be number one to have God help you. Not to help you fight other folks, but to help you when it comes to fighting the devil inside. But you see I don't belong to no church."

"Well, let's you and me have one right off. Two people that help one another to serve God make a church."

I am afraid this ecclesiastical theory will not be considered orthodox. It was Ralph's, and I write it down at the risk of bringing him into condemnation.

But other people before the days of Bud and Ralph have discussed church organization when they should have been doing Christian work. For both of them had forgotten the danger that hung over the old basket-maker, until Shocky burst into the school-house, weeping. In-

87

deed, the poor, nervous little frame was ready to go into convulsions.

"Miss Hawkins——"

Bud started at mention of the name.

"Miss Hawkins has just been over to say that a crowd is going to tar and feather Mr. Pearson to-night. And——" here Shocky wept again. "And he won't run, but he's loaded up the old flintlock, and says he'll die in his tracks."

XVI

The Church Militant

Bud was doubly enlisted on the side of John Pearson, the basket-maker. In the first place, he knew that this perse-cution of the unpopular old man was only a blind to save somebody else; that they were thieves who cried "Stop thief!" And he felt consequently that this was a chance to put his newly-formed resolutions into practice. The Old Testament religious life, which consists in fighting the Lord's enemies, suited Bud's temper and education. It might lead to something better. It was the best possible to him, now. But I am afraid I shall have to acknowledge that there was a second motive that moved Bud to this championship. The good heart of Martha Hawkins hav-ing espoused the cause of the basket-maker, the heart of Bud Means could not help feeling warmly on the same side. Blessed is that man in whose life the driving of duty and the drawing of love impel the same way! But why speak of the driving of duty? For already Bud was learning the better lesson of serving God for the love of God.

The old basket-maker was the most unpopular man in Flat Creek district. He had two great vices. He would go to Clifty and have a "spree" once in three months. And he would tell the truth in a most unscrupulous manner. A man given to plain speaking was quite as objectionable in Flat Creek as he would have been in France under the Empire, the Commune, or the Republic. People who live in glass houses have a horror of people who throw stones. And the old basket-maker, having no friends, was a good scape-goat. In driving him off, Pete Jones would get rid of a dangerous neighbor and divert attention from himself. The immediate crime of the basket-maker was that he had happened to see too much.

"Mr. Hartsook," said Bud, when they got out into the road, "you'd better go straight home to the Squire's. Bekase ef this lightnin' strikes a second time it'll strike awful closte to you. You hadn't better be seen with us. Which way did you come, Shocky?"

"Why, I tried to come down the holler, but I met Jones right by the big road, and he sweared at me and said he'd kill me ef I didn't go back and stay. And so I went back to the house and then slipped out through the graveyard. You see I was bound to come ef I got skinned. For Mr. Pearson's stuck to me and I mean to stick to him, you see."

Bud led Shocky through the graveyard. But when they reached the forest path from the graveyard he thought that perhaps it was not best to "show his hand," as he expressed it, too soon.

"Now, Shocky," he said, "do you run ahead and tell the ole man that I want to see him right off down by the Spring-in-rock. I'll keep closte behind you, and ef anybody offers to trouble you, do you let off a yell and I'll be thar in no time."

When Ralph left the school-house he felt mean. There were Bud and Shocky gone on an errand of mercy, and he, the truant member of the Church of the Best Licks, was not with them. The more he thought of it the more he seemed to be a coward, and the more he despised himself; so, yielding as usual to the first brave impulse he leaped nimbly over the fence and started briskly

90

through the forest in a direction intersecting the path on which were Bud and Shocky. He came in sight just in time to see the first conflict of the Church in the Wilderness with her foes.

For Shocky's little feet went more swiftly on their eager errand than Bud anticipated. He got farther out of Bud's reach than the latter intended he should, and he did not discover Pete Jones until Pete, with his hog-drover's whip, was right upon him.

Shocky tried to halloo for Bud, but he was like one in a nightmare. The yell died into a whisper which could not have been heard ten feet.

I shall not repeat Mr. Jones's words. They were frightfully profane. But he did not stop at words. He swept his whip round and gave little Shocky one terrible cut. Then the voice was released, and the piercing cry of pain brought Bud down the path flying.

"You good-for-nothing scoundrel," growled Bud, "you're a coward and a thief to be a-beatin' a little creetur like him!" and with that Bud walked up on Jones, who prudently changed position in such a way as to get the upper side of the hill.

"Well, I'll gin you the upper side, but come on," cried Bud, "ef you a'n't afeared to fight somebody besides a poor, little, sickly baby or a crippled soldier. Come on!"

Pete was no insignificant antagonist. He had been a great fighter, and his well-seasoned arms were like iron. He had not the splendid set of Bud, but he had more skill and experience in the rude tournament of fists to which the backwoods is so much given. Now, being out of sight of witnesses and sure that he could lie about the fight afterwards, he did not scruple to take advantages which would have disgraced him forever if he had taken them in a public fight on election or training day. He took the uphill side, and he clubbed his whip-stalk, striking Bud with all his force with the heavy end, which, coward-like, he had loaded with lead. Bud threw up his strong left arm and parried the blow, which, however, was so fierce that it fractured one of the bones of the arm. Throwing away his whip he rushed upon Bud furiously, intending to overpower him, but Bud slipped quickly to one side and let Jones pass down the hill, and as Jones came up again Means dealt him one crushing blow that sent him full length upon the ground. Nothing but the leaves saved him from a most terrible fall. Jones sprang to his feet more angry than ever at being whipped by one whom he regarded as a boy, and drew a long dirk-knife. But Pete was blind with rage, and Bud dodged the knife, and this time gave Pete a blow on the nose which marred the homeliness of that feature, and doubled the fellow up against a tree ten feet away.

Ralph came in sight in time to see the beginning of the fight, and he arrived on the ground just as Pete Jones went down under the well-dealt blow from the only remaining fist of Bud Means.

While Ralph tied up Bud's disabled left arm Pete picked himself up slowly, and, muttering that he felt "consid'able shuck up like," crawled away like a whipped puppy. To every one whom he met, Pete, whose intellect seemed to have weakened in sympathy with his frame, remarked feebly that he was consid'able shuck up like, and vouchsafed no other explanation. Even to his wife he only said that he felt purty consid'able shuck up like, and that the boys would have to get on to-night without him. There are some scoundrels whose very malignity is shaken out of them for the time being by a thorough drubbing.

"I'm afraid you're going to have trouble with your arm, Bud," said Ralph tenderly.

"Never mind; I put in my best licks fer *Him*, that air time, Mr. Hartsook." Ralph shivered a little at thought of this, but if it was right to knock Jones down at all, why might not Bud do it "heartily as unto the Lord?" Gideon did not feel any more honest pleasure in chastising the Midianites than did Bud in sending Pete Jones away consid'able shuck up like.

XVII

A Council of War

Shocky, whose feet had flown as soon as he saw the final fall of Pete Jones, told the whole story to the wondering and admiring ears of Miss Hawkins, who unhappily could not remember anything at the East just like it; to the frightened ears of the rheumatic old lady who felt sure her ole man's talk and stubbornness would be the ruin of him, and to the indignant ears of the old soldier who was hobbling up and down, sentinel-wise, in front of his cabin, standing guard over himself.

"No, I won't leave," he said to Ralph and Bud. "You see I jest won't. What would General Winfield Scott say ef he knew that one of them as fit at Lundy's Lane backed out, retreated, run fer fear of a passel of thieves? No, sir, me and the old flintlock will live and die together. I'll put a thunderin' charge of buckshot into the first one of them scoundrels as comes up the holler. It'll be another Lundy's Lane. And you, Mr. Hartsook, may send Scott word that ole Pearson, as fit at Lundy's Lane under him, died a fightin' thieves on Rocky Branch in Hoopole Kyounty, State of Injeanny."

And the old man hobbled faster and faster, taxing his wooden leg to the very utmost, as if his victory depended on the vehemence with which he walked his beat.

Mrs. Pearson sat wringing her hands and looking appealingly at Martha Hawkins, who stood in the door, in despair, looking appealingly at Bud. Bud was stupefied by the old man's stubbornness and his own pain, and in his turn appealed mutely to the master, in whose resources he had boundless confidence. Ralph, seeing that all depended on him, was taxing his wits to think of some way to get round the old man's stubbornness. Shocky hung on to the old man's coat and pulled away at him with many entreating words, but the venerable, bareheaded sentinel strode up and down furiously, with his flintlock on his shoulder and his basket-knife in his belt.

Just at this point somebody could be seen indistinctly through the bushes coming up the hollow.

"Halt!" cried the old hero. "Who goes there?"

"It's me, Mr. Pearson. Don't shoot me, please."

It was the voice of Hannah Thomson. Hearing that the whole neighborhood was rising against the benefactor of Shocky and of her family, she had slipped away from the eyes of her mistress, and ran with breathless haste to give warning in the cabin on Rocky Branch. Seeing Ralph, she blushed, and went into the cabin.

"Well," said Ralph, "the enemy is not coming yet. Let us hold a council of war."

This thought came to Ralph like an inspiration. It pleased the old man's whim, and he sat down on the door-step.

"Now, I suppose," said Ralph, "that General Winfield Scott always looked into things a little before he went into a fight. Didn't he?"

"*To* be sure," assented the old man.

"Well," said Ralph. "What is the condition of the enemy? I suppose the whole neighborhood's against us."

"*To* be sure," said the old man. The rest were silent, but all felt the statement to be about true.

"Next," said Ralph, "I suppose General Winfield Scott would always inquire into the condition of his own troops.

Now let us see. Captain Pearson has Bud, who is the right wing, badly crippled by having his arm broken in the first battle." (Miss Hawkins looked pale.)

"*To* be sure," said the old man.

"And I am the left wing, pretty good at giving advice, but very slender in a fight."

"*To* be sure," said the old man.

"And Shocky and Miss Martha and Hannah good aids, but nothing in a battle."

"*To* be sure," said the basket-maker, a little doubtfully.

"Now, let's look at the arms and accouterments, I think you call them. Well, this old musket has been loaded——"

"This ten year," said the old lady.

"And the lock is so rusty that you could not cock it when you wanted to take aim at Hannah."

The old man looked foolish, and muttered "*To* be sure."

"And there isn't another round of ammunition in the house."

The old man was silent.

"Now let us look at the incumbrances. Here's the old lady and Shocky. If you fight, the enemy will be pleased. It will give them a chance to kill you. And then the old lady will die and they will do with Shocky as they please."

"*To* be sure," said the old man reflectively.

"Now," said Ralph, "General Winfield Scott, under such circumstances, would retreat in good order. Then, when he could muster his forces rightly, he would drive the enemy from his ground."

"To be sure," said the old man. "What ort I to do?"

"Have you any friends?"

"Well, yes; ther's my brother over in Jackson Kyounty. I mout go there."

"Well," said Bud, "do you just go down to Spring-in-rock and stay there. Them folks won't be here tell midnight. I'll come fer you at nine with my roan colt, and I'll set you down over on the big road on Buckeye Run. Then you can git on the mail-wagon that passes there about five o'clock in the mornin', and go over to Jackson County and keep shady till we want you to face the enemy and to swear agin some folks. And then we'll send fer you."

"To be sure," said the old man in a broken voice. "I reckon General Winfield Scott wouldn't disapprove of such a maneuver as that thar."

Miss Martha beamed on Bud to his evident delight, for he carried his painful arm part of the way home with her. Ralph noticed that Hannah looked at *him* with a look full of contending emotions. He read admiration, gratitude, and doubt in the expression of her face, as she turned toward home.

"Well, good by, ole woman," said Pearson, as he took up his little handkerchief full of things and started for his hiding-place; "good by. I didn't never think I'd desart you, and ef the old flintlock hadn't a been rusty, I'd a staid and died right here by the ole cabin. But I reckon 'ta'nt best to be brash." And Shocky looked after him, as he hobbled away over the stones, more than ever convinced that God had forgotten all about things on Flat Creek. He gravely expressed this opinion to the master the next day.

XVIII

Odds and Ends

The Spring-in-rock, or, as it was sometimes, by a curious perversity, called, "the rock-in-spring," was a spring running out of a cavelike fissure in a high limestone cliff. Here the old man sheltered himself on that dreary Christmas evening, until Bud brought his roan colt to the top of the cliff above, and he and Ralph helped the old man up the cliff and into the saddle. Ralph went back to bed, but Bud, who was only too eager to put in his best licks, walked by the side of old John Pearson the six miles over to Buckeye Run, and at last, after eleven o'clock, he deposited him in a hollow sycamore by the road, there to wait the coming of the mail-wagon that would carry him into Jackson County.

"Good by," said the basket-maker, as Bud mounted the colt to return. "Ef I'm wanted jest send me word, and I'll make a forrard movement any time. I don't like this ere thing of running off in the night-time. But I reckon General Winfield Scott would a ordered a retreat ef he'd a been in my shoes. I'm lots obleeged to you. Akordin' to my tell, we're all of us selfish in every thing; but I'll be dog-on'd ef I don't believe you and one or two more is exceptions."

Whether it was that the fact that Pete Jones had got consid'able shuck up demoralized his followers, or whether it was that the old man's flight was suspected, the mob did not turn out in very great force, and the tarring was postponed indefinitely, for by the time they came together it became known somehow that the man with a wooden leg had outrun them all. But the escape of one devoted victim did not mollify the feelings of the people toward the next one.

By the time Bud returned his arm was very painful, and the next day he went under Dr. Small's treatment to reduce the fracture. Whatever suspicions Bud might have of Pete Jones, he was not afflicted with Ralph's dread of the silent young doctor. And if there was anything Small admired, it was physical strength and courage. Small wanted Bud on his side, and least of all did he want him to be Ralph's champion. So that the silent, cool, and skillful doctor went to work to make an impression on Bud Means.

Other influences were at work upon him also. Mrs. Means volleyed and thundered in her usual style about his "takin' up with a one-legged thief, and runnin' arter that master that was a mighty suspicious kind of a customer, akordin' to her tell. She'd allers said so. Ef she'd a been consulted he wouldn't a been hired. He warn't fit company fer nobody."

And old Jack Means 'lowed Bud must want to have *their* barns burnt like some other folks' had been. Fer his part, he had sense enough to know they was some people as it wouldn't do to set a body's self agin. And as fer him, he didn't butt his brains out agin a buckeye-tree. Not when he was sober. And so they managed, during Bud's confinement to the house, to keep him well supplied with all the ordinary discomforts of life.

But one visit from Martha Hawkins, ten words of kindly inquiry from her, and the remark that his broken arm reminded her of something she had seen at the East and something somebody said the time she was to Bosting, were enough to repay the champion a thousand-fold for all that he suffered. Indeed, that visit, and the recollection of Ralph's saying that Jesus Christ was a sort of a Flat Creeker himself, were manna in the wilderness to Bud.

Poor Shocky was sick. The excitement had been too much for him, and though his fever was very slight it was enough to produce just a little delirium. Either Ralph or Miss Martha was generally at the cabin.

"They're coming," said Shocky to Ralph, "they're coming. Pete Jones is agoing to bind me out for a hundred years. I wish Hanner would hold me so's he couldn't. God's forgot all about us here in Flat Creek, and there's nobody to help it."

And he shivered at every sudden sound. He was never free from this delirious fright except when the master held him tight in his arms. He staggered around the floor, the very shadow of Shocky, and was so terrified by the approach of darkness that Ralph staid in the cabin on Wednesday night and Miss Hawkins staid on Thursday night. On Friday, Bud sent a note to Ralph, asking him to come and see him.

"You see, Mr. Hartsook, I ha'n't forgot what we said about puttin' in our best licks for Jesus Christ. I've been a trying to read some about him while I set here. And I read where he said something about doing fer the least of his brethren being all the same like as if it was done fer Jesus Christ hisself. Now there's Shocky. I reckon, p'r'aps, ef anybody is a little brother of Jesus Christ, it is that Shocky. Pete Jones and his brother Bill is detarmined to have him back there to-morry. Bekase, you see, Pete's one of the County Commissioners, and to-morry's the day that they bind out. He wants to bind out that boy jes' to spite ole Pearson and you and me. You see, the ole woman's been helped by the neighbors, and he'll claim Shocky to be a pauper, and they a'n't no human soul here as dares to do a thing contrary to Pete. Couldn't you git him over to Lewisburg? I'll lend you my roan colt."

Ralph thought a minute. He dare not take Shocky to the uncle's where he found his only home. But there was Miss Nancy Sawyer, the old maid who was everybody's blessing. He could ask her to keep him. And, at any rate, he would save Shocky somehow.

As he went out in the dusk, he met Hannah in the lane.

XIX

Face to Face

In the lane, in the dark, under the shadow of the barn,
Ralph met Hannah carrying her bucket of milk (they have
no pails in Indiana). He could see only the white foam
on the milk, and Hannah's white face. Perhaps it was well
that he could not see how white Hannah's face was at
the moment when a sudden trembling made her set down
the heavy bucket. At first neither spoke. The recollection
of all the joy of that walk together in the night came upon
them both. And a great sense of loss made the night seem
supernaturally dark to Ralph. Nor was it any lighter in
the hopeless heart of the bound girl. The presence of
Ralph did not now, as before, make the darkness of her
life light.

"Hannah——" said Ralph presently, and stopped. For
he could not finish the sentence. With a rush there came
upon him a consciousness of the suspicions that filled
Hannah's mind. And with it there came a feeling of guilt.
He saw himself from her stand-point, and felt a remorse
almost as keen as it could have been had he been a criminal. And this sudden and morbid sense of his guilt as it
appeared to Hannah paralyzed him. But when Hannah
lifted her bucket with her hand, and the world with her
heavy heart, and essayed to pass him, Ralph rallied and
said:

"*You* don't believe all these lies that are told about me."

"I don't believe anything, Mr. Hartsook; that is, I don't want to believe anything against you. And I wouldn't mind anything they say if it wasn't for two things—" here she stammered and looked down.

"If it wasn't for what?" said Ralph with a spice of indignant denial in his voice.

Hannah hesitated, but Ralph pressed the question with eagerness.

"I saw you cross that blue-grass pasture the night—the night that you walked home with me." She would have said the night of the robbery, but her heart smote her, and she adopted the more kindly form of the sentence.

Ralph would have explained, but how?

"I did cross the pasture," he began, "but——"

Just here it occurred to Ralph that there was no reason for his night excursion across the pasture. Hannah again took up her bucket, but he said: "Tell me what else you have against me."

"I haven't anything against you. Only I am poor and friendless, and you oughtn't to make my life any heavier. They say that you have paid attention to a great many girls. I don't know why you should want to trifle with me."

Ralph answered her this time. He spoke low. He spoke as though he were speaking to God. "If any man says that I ever trifled with any woman, he lies. I have never loved but one, and you know who that is. And God knows."

"I don't know what to say, Mr. Hartsook." Hannah's voice was broken. These solemn words of love were like a river in the desert, and she was like a wanderer dying of thirst. "I don't know, Mr. Hartsook. If I was alone, it wouldn't matter. But I've got my blind mother and my poor Shocky to look after. And I don't want to make mistakes. And the world is so full of lies I don't know what to

103

believe. Somehow I can't help believing what you say. You seem to speak so true. But——"

"But what?" said Ralph.

"But you know how I saw you just as kind to Martha Hawkins on Sunday as—as——"

"Han—ner!" It was the melodious voice of the angry Mrs. Means, and Hannah lifted her pail and disappeared.

Standing in the shadow of his own despair, Ralph felt how dark a night could be when it had no promise of morning.

And Dr. Small, who had been stabling his horse just inside the barn, came out and moved quietly into the house just as though he had not listened intently to every word of the conversation.

As Ralph walked away he tried to comfort himself by calling to his aid the bull-dog in his character. But somehow it did not do him any good. For what is a bull-dog but a stoic philosopher? Stoicism has its value, but Ralph had come to a place where stoicism was of no account. The memory of the Helper, of his sorrow, his brave and victorious endurance, came when stoicism failed. Happiness might go out of life, but in the light of Christ's life happiness seemed but a small element any how. The love of woman might be denied him, but there still remained what was infinitely more precious and holy, the love of God. There still remained the possibility of heroic living. Working, suffering, and enduring still remained. And he who can work for God and endure for God, surely has yet the best of life left. And, like the knights who could only find the Holy Grail in losing themselves, Hartsook, in throwing his happiness out of the count, found the purest happiness, a sense of the victory of the soul over the tribulations of life. The man who knows this victory scarcely needs the encouragement of the hope of future happiness. There is a real heaven in bravely lifting the load of one's own sorrow and work.

And it was a good thing for Ralph that the danger hanging over Shocky made immediate action necessary.

XX

God Remembers Shocky

At four o'clock the next morning, in the midst of a driving snow, Ralph went timidly up the lane toward the homely castle of the Meanses. He went timidly, for he was afraid of Bull. But he found Bud waiting for him, with the roan colt bridled and saddled. The roan colt was really a large three-year-old, full of the finest sort of animal life, and having, as Bud declared, "a mighty sight of hoss sense fer his age." He seemed to understand at once that there was something extraordinary on hand when he was brought out of his comfortable quarters at four in the morning in the midst of a snow-storm. Bud was sure that the roan colt felt his responsibility.

In the days that followed, Ralph often had occasion to remember this interview with Bud, who had risked much in bringing his fractured arm out into the cold, damp air. Jonathan never clave to David more earnestly than did Bud this December morning to Ralph.

"You see, Mr. Hartsook," said Bud, "I wish I was well myself. It's hard to set still. But it's a-doing me a heap of good. I'm like a boy at school. And I'm a-findin' out that doing one's best licks fer others isn't all they is of it, though it's a good part. I feel like as if I must git Him, you know, to do lots for me. They's always some sums too hard fer a feller, and he has to ax the master to do 'em, you know. But see, the roan's a-stomping round. He wants to be off. Do you know I think that hoss knows something's up? I think he puts in his best licks fer me a good deal better than I do fer Him." There was no more hopeful sign of the growth of a genuine religious life in Bud than the feeling of reverence which caused him to cease to speak too familiarly of God or Christ, and to use pronouns and circumlocutions.

Ralph pressed Bud's right hand. Bud rubbed his face against the colt's nose and said: "Put in your best licks, old fellow." And the colt whinnied. How a horse must want to speak! For Bud was right. Men are gods to horses, and they serve their deities with a faithfulness that shames us.

Then Ralph sprang into the saddle, and the roan, as if wishing to show Bud his willingness, broke into a swinging gallop, and was soon lost from the sight of his master in the darkness and the snow. When Bud could no more hear the sound of the roan's footsteps he returned to the house, to lie awake picturing to himself the journey of Ralph with Shocky and the roan colt. It was a great comfort to Bud that the roan, which was almost a part of himself, represented him in this ride. And he knew the roan well enough to feel sure that he would do credit to his master. "He'll put in his best licks," Bud whispered to himself many a time before daybreak.

The ground was but little frozen, and the snow made the roads more slippery than ever. But the rough-shod roan handled his feet dexterously and with a playful and somewhat self-righteous air, as if he said: "Didn't I do it handsomely that time?" Down slippery hills, through deep mud-holes covered with a slender film of ice, he trod with perfect assurance. And then up over the rough stones of Rocky Hollow, where there was no road at all, he picked his way through the darkness and snow. Ralph could not tell where he was at last, but gave the reins to the roan, who did his duty bravely, and not without a little flourish, as if to show that he had yet plenty of spare power.

A feeble candle-ray, making the dense snow-fall visible, marked for Ralph the site of the basket-maker's cabin. Miss Martha had been admitted to the secret, and had joined in the conspiracy heartily, without being able to recall anything of the kind having occurred at the East, and not remembering having seen or heard of anything of the sort the time she was to Bosting. She had Shocky all ready, having used some of her own capes and shawls to make him warm.

Miss Martha came out to meet Ralph when she heard the feet of the roan before the door.

"O Mr. Hartsook! is that you? What a storm! This is just the way it snows at the East. Shocky's all ready. He didn't know a thing about it tell I waked him this morning. Ever since that he's been saying that God hasn't forgot, after all. It's made me cry more'n once." And Shocky kissed Mrs. Pearson, and told her that when he got away from Flat Creek he'd tell God all about it, and God would bring Mr. Pearson back again. And then Martha Hawkins lifted the frail little form, bundled in shawls, in her arms, and brought him out into the storm; and before she handed him up he embraced her, and said: "O Miss Hawkins! God ha'n't forgot me, after all. Tell Hanner that He ha'n't forgot. I'm going to ask him to git her away from Means's and mother out of the poor-house. I'll ask him just as soon as I get to Lewisburg."

Ralph lifted the trembling form into his arms, and the little fellow only looked up in the face of the master and said: "You see, Mr. Hartsook, I thought God had forgot. But he ha'n't!"

And the words of the little boy comforted the master also. God had not forgotten him either!

From the moment that Ralph took Shocky into his arms, the conduct of the roan colt underwent an entire revolution. Before that he had gone over a bad place with a rush, as though he were ambitious of distinguishing himself by his brilliant execution. Now he trod none the less surely, but he trod tenderly. The neck was no longer arched. He set himself to his work as steadily as though he were twenty years old. For miles he traveled on in a long, swinging walk, putting his feet down carefully and firmly. And Ralph felt the spirit of the colt enter into himself. He cut the snow-storm with his face, and felt a sense of triumph over all his difficulties. The bull-dog's jaws had been his teacher, and now the steady, strong, and conscientious legs of the roan inspired him.

Shocky had not spoken. He lay listening to the steady music of the horse's feet, doubtless framing the footsteps of the roan colt into an anthem of praise to the God who had not forgot. But as the dawn came on, making the snow whiter, he raised himself and said half-aloud, as he watched the flakes chasing one another in whirling eddies, that the snow seemed to be having a good time of it. Then he leaned down again on the master's bosom, full of a still joy, and only roused from his happy reverie to ask what that big, ugly-looking house was.

"See, Mr. Hartsook, how big it is, and how little and ugly the windows is! And the boards is peeling off all over it, and the hogs is right in the front-yard. It don't look just like a house. It looks dreadful. What is it?"

Ralph had dreaded this question. He did not answer it, but asked Shocky to change his position a little, and then he quickened the pace of the horse. But Shocky was a poet, and a poet understands silence more quickly than he does speech. The little fellow shivered as the truth came to him.

"Is that the poor-house?" he said, catching his breath. "Is my mother in that place? *Won't* you take me in there, so as I can just kiss her once? 'Cause she can't see much, you know. And one kiss from me will make her feel so good. And I'll tell her that God ha'n't forgot." He had raised up and caught hold of Ralph's coat.

Ralph had great difficulty in quieting him. He told him that if he went in there Bill Jones might claim that he was a runaway and belonged there. And poor Shocky only shivered and said he was cold. A minute later, Ralph found that he was shaking with a chill, and a horrible dread came over him. What if Shocky should die? It was only a minute's work to get down, take the warm horse-blanket from under the saddle, and wrap it about the boy, then to strip off his own overcoat and add that to it. It was now daylight, and finding, after he had mounted, that Shocky continued to shiver, he put the roan to his best speed for the rest of the way, trotting up and down the slippery hills, and galloping away on the level ground. How bravely the roan laid himself to his work, making the fence-corners fly past in a long procession! But poor little Shocky was too cold to notice them, and Ralph shuddered lest Shocky should never be warm again, and spoke to the roan, and the roan stretched out his head and dropped one ear back to hear the first word of command, and stretched the other forward to look out for danger, and then flew with a splendid speed down the road, past the patches of blackberry briars, past the elderberry bushes, past the familiar red-haw tree in the fence corner, over the bridge without regard to the threat of a five-dollar fine, and at last up the long lane into the village, where the smoke from the chimneys was caught and whirled round with the snow.

XXI

Miss Nancy Sawyer

In a little old cottage in Lewisburg, on one of the streets which was never traveled except by a solitary cow seeking pasture or a countryman bringing wood to some one of the half-dozen families living in it, and which in summer was decked with a profusion of the yellow and white blossoms of the dog-fennel—in this unfrequented street, so generously and unnecessarily broad, lived Miss Nancy Sawyer and her younger sister Semantha. Miss Nancy was a providence, one of those old maids that are benedictions to the whole town; one of those in whom the mother-love, wanting the natural objects on which to spend itself, overflows all bounds and lavishes itself on every needy thing, and grows richer and more abundant with the spending, a fountain of inexhaustible blessing. There is no nobler life possible to any one than to an unmarried woman. The more shame that some choose a selfish one, and thus turn to gall all the affection with which they are endowed. Miss Nancy Sawyer had been Ralph's Sunday-school teacher, and it was precious little, so far as information went, that he learned from her, for she never could conceive of Jerusalem as a place in any essential regard very different from Lewisburg, where she had spent her life. But Ralph learned from her what most Sunday-school teachers fail to teach, the great lesson of Christianity, by the side of which all antiquities and geographies and chronologies and exegetics and other niceties are as nothing.

And now he turned the head of the roan toward the cottage of Miss Nancy Sawyer as naturally as the roan would have gone to his own stall in the stable at home. The snow had gradually ceased to fall, and was eddying round the house, when Ralph dismounted from his foaming horse, and, carrying the still form of Shocky as reverently as though he had been something heavenly, knocked at Miss Nancy Sawyer's door.

With natural feminine instinct that lady started back when she saw Hartsook, for she had just built a fire in the stove, and she now stood at the door with unwashed face and uncombed hair.

"Why, Ralph Hartsook, where did you drop down from —and what have you got?"

"I came from Flat Creek this morning, and I brought you a little angel who has got out of heaven, and needs some of your motherly care."

Shocky was brought in. The chill shook him now by fits only, for a fever had spotted his cheeks already.

"Who are you?" said Miss Nancy, as she unwrapped him.

"I'm Shocky, a little boy as God forgot, and then thought of again."

XXII

Pancakes

Half an hour later, Ralph, having seen Miss Nancy
Sawyer's machinery of warm baths and simple remedies
once safely in operation, and having seen the roan colt
comfortably stabled, and rewarded for his faithfulness
by a bountiful supply of the best hay and the promise of
oats when he was cool—half an hour later Ralph was
doing the most ample, satisfactory, and amazing justice
to his Aunt Matilda's hot buckwheat-cakes and warm
coffee. And after his life in Flat Creek Aunt Matilda's
house did look like paradise. How white the table-cloth,
how bright the coffee-pot, how clean the wood-work, how
glistening the brass door-knobs, how spotless everything
that came under the sovereign sway of Mrs. Matilda
White! For in every Indiana village as large as Lewisburg, there are generally a half-dozen women who are
admitted to be the best housekeepers. All others are only
imitators. And the strife is between these for the pre-
eminence. It it at least safe to say that none in Lewisburg stood so high as an enemy to dirt, and as a "rat,
roach, and mouse exterminator," as did Mrs. Matilda
White, the wife of Ralph's maternal uncle, Robert White,
Esq., a lawyer in successful practice. Of course no member
of Mrs. White's family ever staid at home longer than was
necessary. Her husband found his office—which he kept
in as bad a state as possible in order to maintain an
equilibrium in his life—much more comfortable than the

stiffly clean house at home. From the time that Ralph had
come to live as a chore-boy at his uncle's, he had ever
crossed the threshold of Aunt Matilda's temple of cleanli
ness with a horrible sense of awe. And Walter Johnson
her son by a former marriage, had—poor, weak-willed
fellow!—been driven into bad company and bad habit
by the wretchedness of extreme civilization. And yet he
showed the hereditary trait, for all the genius which
Mrs. White consecrated to the glorious work of making
her house too neat to be habitable, her son Walter gave
to tying exquisite knots in his colored cravats and comb
ing his oiled locks so as to look like a dandy barber. And
she had no other children. The kind Providence that
watches over the destiny of children takes care that very
few of them are lodged in these terribly clean houses.

But Walter was not at the table, and Ralph had so
much anxiety lest his absence should be significant of evil
that he did not venture to inquire after him as he sa
there between Mr. and Mrs. White disposing of Aunt
Matilda's cakes with an appetite only justified by his
long morning ride and the excellence of the brown cakes
the golden honey, and the coffee, enriched, as Aunt
Matilda's always was, with the most generous cream
Aunt Matilda was so absorbed in telling of the doings of
the Dorcas Society that she had entirely forgotten to be
surprised at the early hour of Ralph's arrival. When she
had described the number of the garments finished to
be sent to the Five Points Mission, or the Home for the
Friendless, or the South Sea Islands, I forget which
Ralph thought he saw his chance, while Aunt Matilda
was in a benevolent mood, to broach a plan he had been
revolving for some time. But when he looked at Aunt
Matilda's immaculate—horribly immaculate—housekeep

ing, his heart failed him, and he would have said nothing had she not inadvertently opened the door herself.

"How did you get here so early, Ralph?" and Aunt Matilda's face was shadowed with a coming rebuke.

"By early rising," said Ralph. But, seeing the gathering frown on his aunt's brow, he hastened to tell the story of Shocky as well as he could. Mrs. White did not give way to any impulse toward sympathy until she learned that Shocky was safely housed with Miss Nancy Sawyer.

"Yes, Sister Sawyer has no family cares," she said by way of smoothing her slightly ruffled complacency, "she has no family cares, and she can do those things. Sometimes I think she lets people impose on her and keep her away from the means of grace, and I spoke to our new preacher about it the last time he was here, and asked him to speak to Sister Sawyer about staying away from the ordinances to wait on everybody, but he is a queer man, and he only said that he supposed Sister Sawyer neglected the inferior ordinances that she might attend to higher ones. But I don't see any sense in a minister of the gospel calling prayer-meeting a lower ordinance than feeding the catnip-tea to Mrs. Brown's last baby. But hasn't this little boy—Shocking, or what do you call him?—got any mother?"

"Yes," said Ralph, "and that was just what I was going to say." And he proceeded to tell how anxious Shocky was to see his half-blind mother, and actually ventured to wind up his remarks by suggesting that Shocky's mother be invited to stay over Sunday in Aunt Matilda's house.

"Bless my stars!" said that astounded saint, "fetch a pauper here? What crazy notions you have got! Fetch her here out of the poor-house? Why, she wouldn't be fit to sleep in my——" here Aunt Matilda choked. The bare thought of having a pauper in her billowy beds, whose snowy whiteness was frightful to any ordinary mortal, the bare thought of the contagion of the poor-house taking possession of one of her beds, smothered her. "And then you know sore eyes are very catching."

Ralph boiled a little. "Aunt Matilda, do you think Dorcas was afraid of sore eyes?"

It was a center shot, and the lawyer-uncle, lawyerlike, enjoyed a good hit. And he enjoyed a good hit at his wife best of all, for he never ventured on one himself. But Aunt Matilda felt that a direct reply was impossible. She was not a lawyer but a woman, and so dodged the question by making a counter-charge.

"It seems to me, Ralph, that you have picked up some very low associates. And you go around at night, I am told. You get over here by daylight, and I hear that you have made common cause with a lame soldier who acts as a spy for thieves, and that your running about of nights is likely to get you into trouble."

Ralph was hit this time. "I suppose," he said, "that you've been listening to some of Henry Small's lies."

"Why, Ralph, how you talk! The worst sign of all is that you abuse such a young man as Dr. Small, the most exemplary Christian young man in the county. And he is a great friend of yours, for when he was here last week he did not say a word against you, but looked so sorry when your being in trouble was mentioned. Didn't he, Mr. White?"

Mr. White, as in duty bound, said yes, but he said yes in a cool, lawyerlike way, which showed that he did not take quite so much stock in Dr. Small as his wife did. Which was a comfort to Ralph, who sat picturing to him-

elf the silent flattery which Dr. Small's eyes paid to his
aunt Matilda, and the quiet expression of pain that would
it across his face when Ralph's name was mentioned.
nd never until that moment had Hartsook understood
ow masterful Small's artifices were. He had managed
o elevate himself in Mrs. White's estimation and to de-
troy Ralph at the same time, and had managed to do
oth by a contraction of the eyebrows!

But the silence was growing painful, and Ralph thought
o break it and turn the current of thought from himself
y asking after Mrs. White's son.

"Where is Walter?"

"Oh! Walter's doing well. He went down to Clifty
three weeks ago to study medicine with Henry Small. He
eems so fond of the doctor, and the doctor is such an
xcellent man you know, and I have strong hopes that
Vallie will be led to see the error of his ways by his
ssociation with Henry. I suppose he would have gone to
ee you but for the unfavorable reports that he heard. I
ope, Ralph, you too will make the friendship of Dr.
mall. And for the sake of your poor, dead mother"—
ere Aunt Matilda endeavored to show some emotion—
for the sake of your poor, dead mother——"

But Ralph heard no more. The buckwheat-cakes had
ost their flavor. He remembered that the colt had not
et had his oats, and so, in the very midst of Aunt Ma-
ilda's affecting allusion to his mother, like a stiff-necked
eprobate that he was, Ralph Hartsook rose abruptly
rom the table, put on his hat, and went out toward the
table.

"I declare," said Mrs. White, descending suddenly from
her high moral stand-point, "I declare that boy has stepped
ight on the threshold of the back-door," and she stuffed
her white handkerchief into her pocket, and took down

the floor-cloth to wipe off the imperceptible blemish lef
by Ralph's boot-heels.

And Mr. White followed his nephew to the stable t
request that he would be a little careful what he did abou
anybody in the poor-house, as any trouble with th
Joneses might defeat Mr. White's nomination to th
judgeship of the Court of Common Pleas.

XXIII

A Charitable Institution

When Ralph got back to Miss Nancy Sawyer's, Shocky was sitting up in bed talking to Miss Nancy and Miss Semantha. His cheeks were a little flushed with fever and the excitement of telling his story; theirs were wet with tears.

"Ralph," whispered Miss Nancy, as she drew him into the kitchen, "I want you to get a buggy or a sleigh, and go right over to the poor-house and fetch that boy's mother over here. It'll do me more good than any sermon I ever heard to see that boy in his mother's arms to-morrow. We can keep the old lady over Sunday."

Ralph was delighted, so delighted that he came near kissing good Miss Nancy Sawyer, whose plain face was glorified by her generosity.

But he did not go to the poor-house immediately. He waited until he saw Bill Jones, the Superintendent of the Poor-House, and Pete Jones, the County Commissioner, who was still somewhat shuck up, ride up to the courthouse. Then he drove out of the village, and presently hitched his horse to the poor-house fence, and took a survey of the outside. Forty hogs, nearly ready for slaughter, wallowed in a pen in front of the forlorn and dilapidated house; for though the commissioners allowed a claim for repairs at every meeting, the repairs were never made, and it would not do to scrutinize Mr. Jones's bills too closely, unless you gave up all hope of renomination to office. One curious effect of political aspirations in Hoopole County, was to shut the eyes that they could not see, to close the ears that they could not hear, and to destroy the sense of smell. But Ralph, not being a politician, smelled the hog-pen without and the stench within, and saw everywhere the transparent fraud, and heard the echo of Jones's cruelty.

A weak-eyed girl admitted him, and as he did not wish to make his business known at once, he affected a sort of idle interest in the place, and asked to be allowed to look around. The weak-eyed girl watched him. He found that all the women with children, twenty persons in all, were obliged to sleep in one room, which, owing to the hill-slope, was partly under ground, and which had but half a window for light, and no ventilation, except the chance draft from the door. Jones had declared that the women with children must stay there—"he wan't goin' to have brats a-runnin' over the whole house." Here were vicious women and good women, with their children, crowded like chickens in a coop for market. And there were, as usual in such places, helpless, idiotic women with illegitimate children. Of course this room was the scene of perpetual quarreling and occasional fighting.

In the quarters devoted to the insane, people slightly demented and raving maniacs were in the same rooms, while there were also those utter wrecks which sat in heaps on the floor, mumbling and muttering unintelligible words, the whole current of their thoughts hopelessly muddied, turning around upon itself in eddies never ending.

"That air women," said the weak-eyed girl, "used to holler a heap when she was brought in here. But pap knows how to subjue 'em. He slapped her in the mouth every time she hollered. She don't make no furss now,

but jist sets down that a-way all day, and keeps a-whis-
perin'."

Ralph understood it. When she came in she was the
victim of mania; but she had been beaten into hopeless
idiocy. Indeed this state of incurable imbecility seemed
the end toward which all traveled. Shut in these bare
rooms, with no treatment, no exercise, no variety, and
meager food, cases of slight derangement soon grew into
chronic lunacy.

One young woman, called Phil, a sweet-faced person,
apparently a farmer's wife, came up to Ralph and looked
at him kindly, playing with the buttons on his coat in a
child-like simplicity. Her blue-drilling dress was sewed
all over with patches of white, representing ornamental
buttons, and the womanly instinct toward adornment had
in her taken this childish turn.

"Don't you think they ought to let me go home?" she
said with a sweetness and a wistful, longing, home-sick
look, that touched Ralph to the heart. He looked at her,
and then at the muttering crones, and he could see no
hope of any better fate for her. She followed him round
the barn-like rooms, returning every now and then to
her question, "Don't you think I might go home now?"

The weak-eyed girl had been called away for a moment, and Ralph stood looking into a cell, where there
was a man with a gay red plume in his hat and a strip of
red flannel about his waist. He strutted up and down like
a drill-sergeant.

"I am General Andrew Jackson," he began. "People
don't believe it, but I am. I had my head shot off at Bueny
Visty, and the new one that growed on isn't nigh so good
as the old one; it's tater on one side. That's why they take
advantage of me to shut me up. But I know some things.

My head is tater on one side, but it's all right on t'other.
And when I know a thing in the left side of my head, I
know it. Lean down here. Let me tell you something out
of the left side. Not out of the tater side, mind ye. I
wouldn't a-told you if he hadn't locked me up fer nothing.
Bill Jones is a thief! He sells the bodies of the dead pau-
pers, and then sells the empty coffins back to the county
agin. But that a'n't all——"

Just then the weak-eyed girl came back, and, as Ralph
moved away, General Jackson called out: "That a'n't all.
I'll tell the rest another time. And that a'n't out of the
tater side, you can depend on that. That's out of the left
side. Sound as a nut on that side!"

But Ralph began to wonder where he should find
Hannah's mother.

"Don't go in there!" cried the weak-eyed girl, as Ralph
was opening a door. "Ole Mowley's in there, and she'll
cuss you."

"Oh! well, if that's all, her curses won't hurt," said
Hartsook, pushing open the door. But the volley of
blasphemy and vile language that he received made him
stagger. The old hag paced the floor, abusing everybody
that came in her way. And by the window, in the same
room, feeling the light that struggled through the dusty
glass upon her face, sat a sorrowful intelligent English
woman. Ralph noticed at once that she was English, and
in a few moments he discovered that her sight was de-
fective. Could it be that Hannah's mother was the room-
mate of this loathsome creature, whose profanity and
obscenity did not intermit for a moment?

Happily the weak-eyed girl had not dared to brave the
curses of Mowley. Ralph stepped forward to the woman
by the window, and greeted her.

"Is this Mrs. Thomson?"

"That is my name, sir," she said, turning her face toward Ralph, who could not but remark the contrast between the thorough refinement of her manner and her coarse, scant, unshaped pauper-frock of blue drilling.

"I saw your daughter yesterday."

"Did you see my boy?"

There was a tremulousness in her voice and an agitation in her manner which disclosed the emotion she strove in vain to conceal. For only the day before Bill Jones had informed her that Shocky would be bound out on Saturday, and that she would find that goin' agin him warn't a payin' business, so much as some others he mout mention.

Ralph told her about Shocky's safety. I shall not write down the conversation here. Critics would say that it was an overwrought scene. As if all the world were as cold as they! All I can tell is that this refined woman had all she could do to control herself in her eagerness to get out of her prison-house, away from the blasphemies of Mowley, away from the insults of Jones, away from the sights and sounds and smells of the place, and, above all, her eagerness to fly to the little shocky-head from whom she had been banished for two years. It seemed to her that she could gladly die now, if she could die with that flaxen head upon her bosom.

And so, in spite of the opposition of Bill Jones's son, who threatened her with every sort of evil if she left, Ralph wrapped Mrs. Thomson's blue drilling in Nancy Sawyer's shawl, and bore the feeble woman off to Lewisburg. And as they drove away, a sad, childlike voice cried from the gratings of the upper window, "Good-by! good-by!" Ralph turned and saw that it was Phil, poor Phil, for whom there was no deliverance. And all the way back Ralph pronounced mental maledictions on the

123

Dorcas Society, not for sending garments to the Fiv Points or the South Sea Islands, whichever it was, bu for being so blind to the sorrow and poverty within i reach. He did not know, for he had not read the re ports of the Boards of State Charities, that nearly a alms-houses are very much like this, and that the State New York is not better in this regard than Indiana. An he did not know that it is true in almost all other countie as it was in his own, that "Christian" people do not thin enough of Christ to look for him in these lazar-house

And while Ralph denounced the Dorcas Society, th eager, hungry heart of the mother ran, flew toward th little white-headed boy.

No, I can not do it; I can not tell you about that mee ing. I am sure that Miss Nancy Sawyer's tea tasted e ceedingly good to the pauper, who had known nothing bu cold water for years, and that the bread and butter wer delicious to a palate that had eaten poor-house soup fo dinner, and coarse poor-house bread and vile molasse for supper, and that without change, for three years. Bu I can not tell you how it seemed that evening to Mi Nancy Sawyer, as the poor English lady sat in speechle ectasy, rocking in the old splint-bottomed rocking-cha in the fire-light, while she pressed to her bosom with a the might of her enfeebled arms, the form of the littl Shocky, who half-sobbed and half-sang, over and ove again, "God ha'n't forgot us, mother; God ha'n't forgo us."

XXIV

The Good Samaritan

The Methodist Church to which Mrs. Matilda White and Miss Nancy Sawyer belonged was the leading one in Lewisburg, as it is in most county-seat villages in Indiana. If I may be permitted to express my candid and charitable opinion of the difference between the two women, I shall have to use the old Quaker locution, and say that Miss Sawyer was a Methodist and likewise a Christian; Mrs. White was a Methodist, but I fear she was not likewise.

As to the first part of this assertion, there was no room to doubt Miss Nancy's piety. She could get happy in class-meeting (for who had a better right?), and could witness a good experience in the quarterly love-feast. But it is not upon these grounds that I base my opinion of Miss Nancy. Do not even the Pharisees the same? She never dreamed that she had any right to speak of "Christian Perfection" (which, as Mrs. Partington said of total depravity, is an excellent doctrine if it is lived up to); but when a woman's heart is full of devout affections and good purposes, when her head devises liberal and Christ-like things, when her hands are always open to the poor and always busy with acts of love and self-denial, and when her feet are ever eager to run upon errands of mercy, why, if there be anything worthy of being called Christian Perfection in this world of imperfection, I do not know why such an one does not possess it. What need of analyzing her experiences *in vacuo* to find out the state of her soul?

How Miss Nancy managed to live on her slender income and be so generous was a perpetual source of perplexity to the gossips of Lewisburg. And now that she declared that Mrs. Thomson and Shocky should not return to the poor-house there was a general outcry from the whole Committee of Intermeddlers that she would bring herself to the poor-house before she died. But Nancy Sawyer was the richest woman in Lewisburg, though nobody knew it, and she herself did not once suspect it.

How Miss Nancy and the preacher conspired together and how they managed to bring Mrs. Thomson's case up at the time of the "Sacramental Service" in the afternoon of that Sunday in Lewisburg, and how the preacher made a touching statement of it just before the regular "Collection for the Poor" was taken, and how the warm-hearted Methodists put in dollars instead of dimes while the Presiding Elder read those passages about Zaccheus and other liberal people, and how the congregation sang

"He dies, the Friend of Sinners dies,"

more lustily than ever, after having performed this Christian act—how all this happened I can not take up the reader's time to tell. But I can assure him that the nearly blind English woman did not room with blasphemous old Mowley any more, and that the blue-drilling pauper frock gave way to something better, and that grave little Shocky even danced with delight, and declared that God hadn't forgot, though he'd thought that He had. And Mrs. Matilda White remarked that it was a shame that the collection for the poor at a Methodist sacramental service should be given to a woman who was a member of the Church of England, and like as not never soundly converted!

And Shocky slept in his mother's arms and prayed God not to forget Hannah, while Shocky's mother knit stockings for the store day and night, and day and night she prayed and hoped.

XXV

Bud Wooing

The Sunday that Ralph spent in Lewisburg, the Sunday that Shocky spent in an Earthly Paradise, the Sunday that Mrs. Thomson spent with Shocky instead of old Mowley, the Sunday that Miss Nancy thought was "just like heaven," was also an eventful Sunday with Bud Means. He had long adored Miss Martha in his secret heart, but, like many other giants, while brave enough to face and fight dragons, he was a coward in the presence of the woman that he loved. Let us honor him for it. The man who loves a woman truly, reverences her profoundly, and feels abashed in her presence. The man who is never abashed in the presence of womanhood, the man who tells his love without a tremor, is a heartless, shallow egotist. Bud's nature was not fine. But it was deep, true, and manly. To him Martha Hawkins was the chief of women. What was he that he should aspire to possess her?

And yet on that Sunday, with his crippled arm carefully bound up, with his cleanest shirt, and with his heavy boots freshly oiled with the fat of the raccoon, he started hopefully through fields white with snow to the house of Squire Hawkins. When he started his spirits were high, but they descended exactly in proportion to his proximity to the object of his love. He thought himself not dressed well enough. He wished his shoulders were not so square, and his arms not so stout. He wished that he had booklarnin' enough to court in nice, big words. And so, by recounting his own deficiencies, he succeeded in making himself feel weak, and awkward, and generally good-for-nothing, by the time he walked up between the rows of dead hollyhocks to the Squire's front door, to tap at which took all his remaining strength.

Miss Martha received her perspiring lover most graciously, but this only convinced Bud more than ever that she was a superior being. If she had slighted him a bit, so as to awaken his combativeness a little, his bashfulness would have disappeared.

It was in vain that Martha inquired about his arm and complimented his courage. Bud could only think of his big feet, his clumsy hands, and his slow tongue. He answered in monosyllables, using his red silk handkerchief diligently.

"Is your arm improving?" asked Miss Hawkins.

"Yes, I think it is," said Bud, hastily crossing his right leg over his left, and trying to get his fists out of sight.

"Have you heard from Mr. Pearson?"

"No, I ha'n't," answered Bud, removing his right foot to the floor again, because it looked so big, and trying to push his left hand into his pocket.

"Beautiful sunshine, isn't?" said Martha.

"Yes, 'tis," answered Bud, sticking his right foot up on the rung of the chair and putting his right hand behind him.

"This snow looks like the snow we have at the East," said Martha. "It snowed that way the time I was to Bosting."

"Did it?" said Bud, not thinking of the snow at all, nor of Boston, but thinking how much better he would have appeared had he left his arms and legs at home.

"I suppose Mr. Hartsook rode your horse to Lewisburg?"

"Yes, he did"; and Bud hung both hands at his side.

"You were very kind."

This set Bud's heart a-going so that he could not say anything, but he looked eloquently at Miss Hawkins, drew both feet under the chair, and rammed his hands into his pockets. Then, suddenly remembering how awkward he must look, he immediately pulled his hands out again, and crossed his legs. There was a silence of a few minutes, during which Bud made up his mind to do the most desperate thing he could think of—to declare his love and take the consequences.

"You see, Miss Hawkins," he began, forgetting boots and fists in his agony, "I thought as how I'd come over here to-day, and"—but here his heart failed him utterly— "and—see—you."

"I'm glad to see you, Mr. Means."

"And I thought I'd tell you"—Martha was sure it was coming now, for Bud was in dead earnest—"and I thought I'd just like to tell you, ef I only know'd jest how to tell it right"—here Bud got frightened, and did not dare close the sentence as he had intended—"I thought as how you might like to know—or ruther I wanted to tell you—that —the—that I—that we—all of us—think—that I—that we are going to have a spellin'-school a Chewsday night."

"I'm real glad to hear it," said the bland but disappointed Martha. "We used to have spelling-schools at the East." But Miss Martha could not remember that they had them "to Bosting."

Hard as it is for a bashful man to talk, it is still more difficult for him to close the conversation. Most men like to leave a favorable impression, and a bashful man is always waiting with the forlorn hope that some favorable turn in the talk may let him out without absolute discomfiture. And so Bud stayed a long time, and how he ever did get away he never could tell.

XXVI

A Letter and Its Consequences

"Squar Haukins

"this is too Lett u no that u beter be Keerful hoo yoo an yore familly tacks cides with fer peepl wont Stan it too hev the Men wat's sportin the wuns wat's robin us, sported bi yor Fokes kepin kumpne with 'em, u been a ossifer ov the Lau, yor Ha wil bern as qick as to an yor Barn tu. so Tak kere. No mor ad pressnt."

This letter accomplished its purpose. The squire's spectacles slipped off several times while he read it. His wig had to be adjusted. If he had been threatened personally he would not have minded it so much. But the hay-stacks were dearer to him than the apple of his glass eye. The barn was more precious than his wig. And those who hoped to touch Bud in a tender place through this letter knew the Squire's weakness far better than they knew the spelling-book. To see his new red barn with its large "Mormon" hay-press inside, and the mounted Indian on the vane, consumed, was too much for the Hawkins heart to stand. Evidently the danger was on the side of his niece. But how should he influence Martha to give up Bud? Martha did not value the hay-stacks half so highly as she did her lover. Martha did not think the new red barn, with the great Mormon press inside and the galloping Indian on the vane, worth half so much as a moral principle or a kind-hearted action. Martha, bless her! would have sacrificed anything rather than forsake the poor. But Squire Hawkins's lips shut tight over his false teeth in a way that suggested astringent purse-strings, and Squire Hawkins could not sleep at night if the new red barn, with the galloping Indian on the vane, were in danger. Martha must be reached some how.

So, with many adjustings of that most adjustable wig, with many turnings of that reversible glass eye, the squire managed to frighten Martha by the intimation that he had been threatened, and to make her understand, what it cost her much to understand, that she must turn the cold shoulder to chivalrous, awkward Bud, whom she loved most tenderly, partly, perhaps, because he did not remind her of anybody she knew at the East.

Tuesday evening was the fatal time. Spelling-school was the fatal occasion. Bud was the victim. Pete Jones had his revenge. For Bud had been all the evening trying to muster courage enough to offer himself as Martha's escort. He was not encouraged by the fact that he had spelled even worse than usual, while Martha had distinguished herself by holding her ground against Jeems Phillips for half an hour. But he screwed his courage to the sticking place, not by quoting to himself the adage, "Faint heart never won fair lady," which, indeed, he had never heard, but by reminding himself that "ef you don't resk nothin' you'll never git nothin'." So, when the spelling-school had adjourned, he sidled up to her, and, looking dreadfully solemn and a little foolish, he said:

"Kin I see you safe home?"

And she, with a feeling that her uncle's life was in danger, and that his salvation depended upon her resolution—she, with a feeling that she was pronouncing sentence of death on her own great hope, answered huskily:

"No, I thank you."

If she had only known that it was the red barn with the Indian on top that was in danger, she would probably have let the galloping brave take care of himself.

It seemed to Bud, as he walked home mortified, disgraced, disappointed, hopeless, that all the world had gone down in a whirlpool of despair.

"Might a knowed it," he said to himself. "Of course, a smart gal like Martha a'n't agoin' to take a big, blunderin' fool that can't spell in two syllables. What's the use of tryin'? A Flat Cricker is a Flat Cricker. You can't make nothin' else out of him, no more nor you can make a China hog into a Berkshire."

XXVII

A Loss and a Gain

Dr. Small, silent, attentive, assiduous Dr. Small, set him
self to work to bind up the wounded heart of Bud Means
even as he had bound up his broken arm. The flattery o
his fine eyes, which looked at Bud's muscles so admir
ingly, which gave attention to his lightest remark, wa
not lost on the young Flat Creek Hercules. Outwardly
at least Pete Jones showed no inclination to revenge him
self on Bud. Was it respect for muscle, or was it the in
fluence of Small? At any rate, the concentrated extrac
of the resentment of Pete Jones and his clique was now
ready to empty itself upon the head of Hartsook. And
Ralph found himself in his dire extremity without ever
the support of Bud, whose good resolutions seemed t
give way all at once. There have been many men of cul
ture and more favorable surroundings who have throw
themselves away with less provocation. As it was, Bud
quit school, avoided Ralph, and seemed more than eve
under the influence of Dr. Small, besides becoming th
intimate of Walter Johnson, Small's student and Mrs
Matilda White's son. They made a strange pair—Bud wit
his firm jaw and silent, cautious manner, and Walte
Johnson with his weak chin, his nice cravat-ties, and gen
eral dandy appearance.

To be thus deserted in his darkest hour by his onl
friend was the bitterest ingredient in Ralph's cup. I
vain he sought an interview. Bud always eluded him

While by all the faces about him Ralph learned that the storm was getting nearer and nearer to himself. It might delay. If it had been Pete Jones alone, it might blow over. But Ralph felt sure that the relentless hand of Dr. Small was present in all his troubles. And he had only to look into Small's eye to know how inextinguishable was a malignity that burned so steadily and so quietly.

But there is no cup of unmixed bitterness. With an innocent man there is no night so dark that some star does not shine. Beside his religious faith Ralph had one strong sheet-anchor. On his return from Lewisburg on Monday Bud had handed him a note, written on common blue foolscap, in round, old-fashioned hand. It ran:

"Dear Sir: Anybody who can do so good a thing as you did for our Shocky, can not be bad. I hope you will forgive me. All the appearances in the world, and all that anybody says, can not make me think you anything else but a good man. I hope God will reward you. You must not answer this, and you hadn't better see me again, or think any more of what you spoke about the other night. I shall be a slave for three years more, and then I must work for my mother and Shocky; but I felt so bad to think that I had spoken so hard to you, that I could not help writing this. Respectfully,

HANNAH THOMSON"
"To MR. R. HARTSOOK, ESQ."

Ralph read it over and over. What else he did with it I shall not tell. You want to know if he kissed it, and put it in his bosom. Many a man as intelligent and manly as Hartsook has done quite as foolish a thing as that. You have been a little silly perhaps—if it is silly—and you have acted in a sentimental sort of a way over such things.

135

But it would never do for me to tell you what Ralph did. Whether he put the letter in his bosom or not, he put the words in his heart, and, metaphorically speaking, he shook that little blue billet, written on coarse foolscap paper— he shook that little letter, full of confidence, in the face and eyes of all the calamities that haunted him. If Hannah believed in him, the whole world might distrust him. When Hannah was in one scale and the whole world in the other, of what account was the world? Justice may be blind, but all the pictures of blind cupids in the world can not make Love blind. And it was well that Ralph weighed things in this way. For the time was come in which he needed all the courage the blue billet could give him.

XXVIII

The Flight

About ten days after Ralph's return to Flat Creek things came to a crisis.

The master was rather relieved at first to have the crisis come. He had been holding juvenile Flat Creek under his feet by sheer force of will. And such an exercise of "psychic power" is very exhausting. In racing on the Ohio the engineer sometimes sends the largest of the firemen to hold the safety-valve down, and this he does by hanging himself to the lever by his hands. Ralph felt that he had been holding the safety-valve down, and that he was so weary of the operation that an explosion would be a real relief. He was a little tired of having everybody look at him as a thief. It was a little irksome to know that new bolts were put on the doors of the houses in which he had staid. And now that Shocky was gone, and Bud had turned against him, and Aunt Matilda suspected him, and even poor, weak, exquisite Walter Johnson would not associate with him, he felt himself an outlaw indeed. He would have gone away to Texas or the new gold-fields in California had it not been for one thing. That letter on blue foolscap paper kept a little warmth in his heart.

His course from school on the evening that something happened lay through the sugar-camp. Among the dark trunks of the maples, solemn and lofty pillars, he debated the case. To stay, or to flee? The worn nerves could not keep their present tension much longer.

It was just by the brook, or, as they say in Indiana, the "branch," that something happened which brought him to a sudden decision. Ralph never afterward could forget that brook. It was a swift-running little stream, that did not babble blatantly over the stones. It ran through a thicket of willows, through the sugar-camp, and out into Means's pasture. Ralph had just passed through the thicket, had just crossed the brook on the half-decayed log that spanned it, when, as he emerged from the water-willows on the other side, he started with a sudden shock. For there was Hannah, with a white, white face, holding out a little note folded like an old-fashioned thumb-paper.

"Go quick!" she stammered as she slipped it into Ralph's hand, inadvertently touching his fingers with her own— a touch that went tingling through the school-master's nerves. But she had hardly said the words until she was gone down the brookside path and over into the pasture. A few minutes afterward she drove the cows up into the lot and meekly took her scolding from Mrs. Means for being gone sech an awful long time, like a lazy, good-fer-nothin' piece of goods that she was.

Ralph opened the thumb-paper note, written on a page torn from an old copy-book, in Bud's "hand-write" and running:

"Mr. Heartsook
        "deer Sur:
    "i Put in my best licks, taint no use. Run fer yore life. A plans on foot to tar an fether or wuss to-night. Go rite off. Things is awful juberous.   Bud."

The first question with Ralph was whether he could depend on Bud. But he soon made up his mind that treachery of this sort was not one of his traits. He had mourned over the destruction of Bud's good resolutions

138

by Martha Hawkins's refusal, and being a disinterested party he could have comforted Bud by explaining Martha's "mitten." But he felt sure that Bud was not treacherous. It was a relief, then, as he stood there to know that the false truce was over, and worst had come to worst.

His first impulse was to stay and fight. But his nerves were not strong enough to execute so foolhardy a resolution. He seemed to see a man behind every maple-trunk. Darkness was fast coming on, and he knew that his absence from supper at his boarding-place could not fail to excite suspicion. There was no time to be lost. So he started.

Let one once start to run from a danger, and panic is apt to ensue. The forests, the stalk-fields, the dark hollows through which he passed, seemed to be peopled with terrors. He knew Small and Jones well enough to know that every avenue of escape would be carefully picketed. So there was nothing to do but to take the shortest path to the old trysting-place, the Spring-in-rock.

Here he sat and shook with terror. Mad with himself, he inly denounced himself for a coward. But the effect was really a physical one. The chill and panic now were the reaction from the previous strain.

For when the sound of his pursuers' voices broke upon his ears early in the evening, Ralph shook no more; the warm blood set back again toward the extremities, and his self-control returned when he needed it. He gathered some stones about him, as the only weapons of defense at hand. The mob was on the cliff above. But he thought that he heard footsteps in the bed of the creek below. If this were so, there could be no doubt that his hiding-place was suspected.

"O Hank!" shouted Bud from the top of the cliff to

some one in the creek below, "be sure to look at the Spring-in-rock—I think he's there."

This hint was not lost on Ralph, who speedily changed his quarters by climbing up to a secluded, shelflike ledge above the spring. He was none too soon, for Pete Jones and Hank Banta were soon looking all around the spring for him, while he held a twenty-pound stone over their heads ready to drop upon them in case they should think of looking on the ledge above.

When the crowd were gone Ralph knew that one road was open to him. He could follow down the creek to Clifty, and thence he might escape. But, traveling down to Clifty, he debated whether it was best to escape. To flee was to confess his guilt, to make himself an outlaw, to put an insurmountable barrier between himself and Hannah, whose terror-stricken and anxious face as she stood by the brook-willows haunted him now, and was an involuntary witness to her love.

Long before he reached Clifty his mind was made up not to flee another mile. He knocked at the door of Squire Underwood. But Squire Underwood was also a doctor, and had been called away. He knocked at the door of Squire Doolittle. But Squire Doolittle had gone to Lewisburg. He was about to give up all hope of being able to surrender himself to the law when he met Squire Hawkins, who had come over to Clifty to avoid responsibility for the ill-deeds of his neighbors which he was powerless to prevent.

"Is that you, Mr. Hartsook?"

"Yes, and I want you to arrest me and try me here in Clifty."

XXIX

The Trial

he "prosecuting attorney" (for so the State's attorney
called in Indiana) had been sent for the night before.
alph refused all legal help. It was not wise to reject
ounsel, but all his blood was up, and he declared that
e would not be cleared by legal quibbles. If his in-
ocence were not made evident to everybody, he would
ather not be acquitted on a preliminary examination.
Ie would go over to the circuit court and have the
natter sifted to the bottom. But he would have been
leased had his uncle offered him counsel, though he
ould have declined it. He would have felt better to
ave had a letter from home somewhat different from
ne one he received from his Aunt Matilda by the hand
f the prosecuting attorney. It was not very encouraging
r very sympathetic, though it was very characteristic.

Dear Ralph:
"This is what I have always been afraid of. I warned
ou faithfully the last time I saw you. My skirts are
lear of your blood. I can not consent for your uncle to
ppear as your counsel or go to your bail. You know
ow much it would injure him in the county, and he has
o right to suffer for your evil acts. O my dear nephew!
or the sake of your poor, dead mother——"

We never shall know what the rest of that letter was.
Vhenever Aunt Matilda got to Ralph's poor, dead mother

141

in her conversation, Ralph ran out of the house. And now that his poor, dead mother was again made to do servic in his aunt's pious rhetoric, he landed the letter on th hot coals before him, and watched it vanish into smok with a grim satisfaction.

Ralph was a little afraid of a mob. But Clifty wa better than Flat Creek, and Squire Hawkins, with all h faults, loved justice, and had a profound respect for th majesty of the law, and a profound respect for his ow majesty when sitting as a court representing the law Whatever maneuvers he might resort to in business affai in order to avoid a conflict with his lawless neighbor he was courageous and inflexible on the bench. Th Squire was the better part of him. With the co-operatic of the constable, he had organized a *posse* of men wh could be depended on to enforce the law against a mo

By the time the trial opened in the large school-hou in Clifty at eleven o'clock, all the surrounding count had emptied its population into Clifty, and all Flat Cree was on hand ready to testify to something. Those wh knew the least appeared to know the most, and wer prodigal of their significant winks and nods. Mrs. Mea had always suspected him. She seed some mighty susp cious things about him from the word go. She'd alle had her doubts whether he was jist the thing, and ef h ole man had axed her, liker-n not he never'd a be hired. She'd seed things with her own livin' eyes th beat all she ever seed in all her born days. And Pete Jon said he'd allers knowed ther warn't no good in sech feller. Couldn't stay abed when he got there. And Gran Sanders said, Law sakes! nobody'd ever a-found him o ef it hadn't been fer her. Didn't she go all over t neighborhood a-warnin' people? Fer her part, she se straight through that piece of goods. He was fond of the gals, too! Nothing was so great a crime in her eyes as to be fond of the gals.

The constable paid unwitting tribute to William the Conqueror by crying Squire Hawkins's court open with an Oyez! or, as he said it, "O yes!" and the Squire asked Squire Underwood, who came in at that minute, to sit with him. From the start, it was evident to Ralph that the prosecuting attorney had been thoroughly posted by Small, though, looking at that worthy's face, one would have thought him the most disinterested and philosophical spectator in the court-room.

Bronson, the prosecutor, was a young man, and this was his first case since his election. He was very ambitious to distinguish himself, very anxious to have Flat Creek influence on his side in politics; and, consequently, he was very determined to send Ralph Hartsook to State prison, justly or unjustly, by fair means or foul. To his professional eyes this was not a question of right and wrong, not a question of life or death to such a man as Ralph. It was George H. Bronson's opportunity to distinguish himself. And so, with many knowing and confident nods and hints, and with much deference to the two squires, he opened the case, affecting great indignation at Ralph's wickedness, and uttering Delphic hints about striped pants and shaven head, and the grating of prison-doors at Jeffersonville.

"And, now, if the court please, I am about to call a witness whose testimony is very important indeed. Mrs. Sarah Jane Means will please step forward and be sworn."

This Mrs. Means did with alacrity. She had met the prosecutor, and impressed him with her dark hints. She was sworn.

"Now, Mrs. Means, have the goodness to tell us what you know of the robbery at the house of Peter Schroeder, and the part defendant had in it."

"Well, you see, I allers suspected that air young man——"

Here Squire Underwood stopped her, and told her that she must not tell her suspicions, but facts.

"Well, it's facts I am a-going to tell," she sniffed indignantly. "It's facts that I mean to tell." Here her voice rose to a keen pitch, and she began to abuse the defendant. Again and again the court insisted that she must tell what there was suspicious about the school-master. At last she got it out.

"Well, fer one thing, what kind of gals did he go with? Hey? Why, with my bound gal, Hanner, a loafin' along through the blue-grass paster at ten o'clock, and keepin' that gal that's got no protector but me out that a-way, and destroyin' her character by his company, that a'n't fit fer nobody."

Here Bronson saw that he had caught a tartar. He said he had no more questions to ask of Mrs. Means, and that, unless the defendant wished to cross-question her, she could stand aside. Ralph said he would like to ask her one question.

"Did I ever go with your daughter Miranda?"

"No, you didn't," answered the witness, with a tone and a toss of the head that let the cat out, and set the court-room in a giggle. Bronson saw that he was gaining nothing, and now resolved to follow the line which Small had indicated.

Pete Jones was called, and swore point-blank that he heard Ralph go out of the house soon after he went to bed, and that he heard him return at two in the morning. This testimony was given without hesitation, and made

144

great impression against Ralph in the minds of the ustices. Mrs. Jones, a poor, brow-beaten woman, came on he stand in a frightened way, and swore to the same lies s her husband. Ralph cross-questioned her, but her part ad been well learned.

There seemed now little hope for Ralph. But just at his moment who should stride into the school-house but Pearson, the one-legged, old-soldier basket-maker? He ad crept home the night before, "to see ef the ole woman lidn't want somethin'," and hearing of Ralph's arrest, he concluded that the time for him to make "a forrard movement" had come, and so he determined to face the foe.

"Looky here, Squar," he said, wiping the perspiration om his brow, "looky here. I jest want to say that I kin ell as much about this case as anybody."

"Let us hear it, then," said Bronson, who thought he would nail Ralph now for certain.

So, with many allusions to the time he fit at Lundy's Lane, and some indignant remarks about the pack of hieves that driv him off, and a passing tribute to Miss Martha Hawkins, and sundry other digressions, in which he had to be checked, the old man told how he'd drunk whisky at Welch's store that night, and how Welch's whisky was all-fired mean, and how it allers went straight o his head, and how he had got a leetle too much, and how he had felt kyinder gin aout by the time he got to he blacksmith's shop, an' how he had laid down to rest, and how as he s'posed the boys had crated him, and how he thought it war all-fired mean to crate a old soldier what fit the Britishers, and lost his leg by one of the blamed critters a punchin' his bagonet through it; and how when he woke up it was all-fired cold, and how he olled off the crate and went on towards home, and how when he got up to the top of Means's hill he met Pete

Jones and Bill Jones, and a slim sort of a young man,
ridin'; and how he know'd the Joneses by ther hosses, a
some more things of that kyind about 'em; but he did
know the slim young man, tho' he tho't he might tell h
ef he seed him agin, kase he was dressed up so slick a
town-like. But blamed ef he didn't think it hard that
passel of thieves sech as the Joneses should try to p
ther mean things on to a man like the master, that w
so kyind to him and to Shocky, tho', fer that matt
blamed ef he didn't think we was all selfish, akordin
his tell. Had seed somebody that night a crossin' ov
the blue-grass paster. Didn't know who in thunder 'tw
but it was somebody a makin' straight fer Pete Jone
Hadn't seed nobody else, 'ceptin' Dr. Small, a short wa
behind the Joneses.

Hannah was now brought on the stand. She was grea
agitated, and answered with much reluctance. Lived
Mr. Means's. Was eighteen years of age in October. H
been bound to Mrs. Means three years ago. Had walk
home with Mr. Hartsook that evening, and, happeni
to look out of the window toward morning, she saw so
one cross the pasture. Did not know who it was. Thoug
it was Mr. Hartsook. Here Mr. Bronson (evident
prompted by a suggestion that came from what Sm
had overheard when he listened in the barn) asked h
if Mr. Hartsook had ever said anything to her about t
matter afterward. After some hesitation, Hannah sa
that he had said that he crossed the pasture. Of his ov
accord? No, she spoke of it first. Had Mr. Hartsook offer
any explanations? No, he hadn't. Had he ever paid h
any attention afterward? No. Ralph declined to cro
question Hannah. To him she never seemed so fair
when telling the truth so sublimely.

Bronson now informed the court that this little tri

of having the old soldier happen in, in the nick of time, wouldn't save the prisoner at the bar from the just punishment which an outraged law visited upon such crimes as his. He regretted that his duty as a public prosecutor caused it to fall to his lot to marshal the evidence that was to blight the prospects and blast the character; and annihilate for ever, so able and promising a young man, but that the law knew no difference between the educated and the uneducated, and that for his part he thought Hartsook a most dangerous foe to the peace of society. The evidence already given fastened suspicion upon him. The prisoner had not yet been able to break its force at all. The prisoner had not even dared to try to explain the reason for his being out at night to a young lady. He would now conclude by giving the last touch to the dark evidence that would sink the once fair name of Ralph Hartsook in a hundred fathoms of infamy. He would ask that Henry Banta be called.

Hank came forward sheepishly, and was sworn. Lived about a hundred yards from the house that was robbed. He seen ole man Pearson and the master and one other feller that he didn't know come away from there together about one o'clock. He heerd the horses kickin', and went out to the stable to see about them. He seed two men come out of Schroeder's backdoor and meet one man standing at the gate. When they got closter he knowed Pearson by his wooden leg and the master by his hat. On cross-examination he was a little confused when asked why he hadn't told of it before, but said that he was afraid to say much, bekase the folks was a talkin' about hanging the master, and he didn't want no lynchin'.

The prosecution here rested, Bronson maintaining that there was enough evidence to justify Ralph's committal

to await trial. But the court thought that as the defend
ant had no counsel and offered no rebutting testimony
it would be only fair to hear what the prisoner had t
say in his own defense.

All this while poor Ralph was looking about the room
for Bud. Bud's actions had of late been strangely con
tradictory. But had he turned coward and deserted h
friend? Why else did he avoid the session of the court
After asking himself such questions as these, Ralph woul
wonder at his own folly. What could Bud do if he wer
there? There was no human power that could prevent th
victim of so vile a conspiracy as this, lodging in tha
worst of State Prisons at Jeffersonville, a place too ba
for criminals. But when there is no human power to help
how naturally does the human mind look for some inter
vention of God on the side of Right! and Ralph's faith i
Providence looked in the direction of Bud. But since n
Bud came, he shut down the valves and rose to his fee
proudly, defiantly, fiercely calm.

"It's of no use for me to say anything. Peter Jones ha
sworn to a deliberate falsehood, and he knows it. He ha
made his wife perjure her poor soul that she dare not ca
her own." Here Pete's fists clenched, but Ralph in hi
present humor did not care for mobs. The spirit of th
bull-dog had complete possession of him. "It is of n
use for me to tell you that Henry Banta has sworn to
lie, partly to revenge himself on me for sundry punish
ments I have given him, and partly, perhaps, for money
The real thieves are in this courtroom. I could put m
finger on them."

"*To* be sure," responded the old basket-maker. Ralp
looked at Pete Jones, then at Small. The fiercely cal
look attracted the attention of the people. He knew tha
this look would probably cost him his life before th

148

xt morning. But he did not care for life. "The testimony
Miss Hannah Thomson is every word true. I believe
at of Mr. Pearson to be true. The rest is false. But I can
t prove it. I know the men I have to deal with. I shall
t escape with State prison. They will not spare my life.
it the people of Clifty will one day find out who are
e thieves." Ralph then proceeded to tell how he had
ft Pete Jones's, Mr. Jones's bed being uncomfortable;
w he had walked through the pasture; how he had
en three men on horseback; how he had noticed the
rrel with the white left forefoot and white nose; how
 had seen Dr. Small; how, after his return, he had
ard some one enter the house, and how he had rec-
nized the horse the next morning. "There," said Ralph
sperately, leveling his finger at Pete, "there is a man
ho will yet see the inside of a penitentiary. I shall not
e to see it, but the rest of you will." Pete quailed.
lph's speech could not of course break the force of
e testimony against him. But it had its effect, and it
d effect enough to alarm Bronson, who rose and said:
"I should like to ask the prisoner at the bar one ques-
n."

"Ask me a dozen," said Hartsook, looking more like a
ng than a criminal.

"Well, then, Mr. Hartsook. You need not answer unless
u choose; but what prompted you to take the direction
u did in your walk on that evening?"

This shot brought Ralph down. To answer this ques-
n truly would attach to friendless Hannah Thomson
me of the disgrace that now belonged to him.

"I decline to answer," said Ralph.

"Of course, I do not want the prisoner to criminate
mself," said Bronson significantly.

During this last passage Bud had come in, but, to

Ralph's disappointment he remained near the door, tall
ing to Walter Johnson, who had come with him. Th
magistrates put their heads together to fix the amoun
of bail, and, as they differed, talked for some minute
Small now for the first time thought best to make a mov
in his own proper person. He could hardly have bee
afraid of Ralph's acquittal. He may have been a littl
anxious at the manner in which he had been mentioned
and at the significant look of Ralph, and he probabl
meant to excite indignation enough against the schoo
master to break the force of his speech, and secure th
lynching of the prisoner, chiefly by people outside h
gang. He rose, and asked the court in gentlest tones t
hear him. He had no personal interest in this trial, excep
his interest in the welfare of his old schoolmate, M
Hartsook. He was grieved and disappointed to find th
evidence against him so damaging, and he would not fc
the world add a feather to it, if it were not that his ow
name had been twice alluded to by the defendant, an
by his friend, and perhaps his confederate, John Pearso
He was prepared to swear that he was not over in Fl
Creek the night of the robbery later than ten o'clock, an
while the statements of the two persons alluded t
whether maliciously intended or not, could not implica
him at all, he thought perhaps this lack of veracity i
their statements might be of weight in determining som
other points. He therefore suggested—he could onl
suggest, as he was not a party to the case in anyway—
that his student, Mr. Walter Johnson, be called to testif
as to his—Dr. Small's—exact whereabouts on the nigh
in question. They were together in his office until tw
when he went to the tavern and went to bed.

Squire Hawkins, having adjusted his teeth, his wig, an
his glass eye, thanked Dr. Small for a suggestion so valu

le, and thought best to put John Pearson under arrest
efore proceeding further. Mr. Pearson was therefore
rested, and was heard to mutter something about a
assel of thieves," when the court warned him to be
uiet.

Walter Johnson was then called. But before giving his
estimony, I must crave the reader's patience while I go
ack to some things which happened nearly a week be-
re, and which will serve to make it intelligible.

XXX

"Brother Sodom"

In order to explain Walter Johnson's testimony and his
state of mind, I must carry the reader back nearly a week.
The scene was Dr. Small's office. Bud and Walter Johnson had been having some confidential conversation that
evening, and Bud had gotten more out of his companion
than that exquisite but weak young man had intended. He
looked round in a frightened way.

"You see," said Walter, "if Small knew I had told you
that, I'd get a bullet some night from somebody. But
when you're initiated it'll be all right. Sometimes I wish
I was out of it. But, you know, Small's this kind of a man.
He sees through you. He can look through a door"—and
here he shivered, and his voice broke down into a whisper. But Bud was perfectly cool, and doubtless it was
the strong coolness of Bud that made Walter, who shuddered at a shadow, come to him for sympathy and un-
bosom himself of one of his guilty secrets.

"Let's go and hear Brother Sodom preach to-night,"
said Bud.

"No, I don't like to."

"He don't scare you?" There was just a touch of ridi-
cule in Bud's voice. He knew Walter, and he had not
counted amiss when he used this little goad to prick a
skin so sensitive. "Brother Sodom" was the nickname
given by scoffers to the preacher—Mr. Soden—whose

152

manner of preaching had so aroused Bud's combativeness, and whose saddle-stirrups Bud had helped to amputate. For reasons of his own, Bud thought best to subject young Johnson to the heat of Mr. Soden's furnace.

Peter Cartwright boasts that, on a certain occasion, he "shook his brimstone wallet" over the people. Mr. Soden could never preach without his brimstone wallet. There are those of a refinement so attenuated that they will not admit that fear can have any place in religion. But a religion without fear could never have evangelized or civilized the West, which at one time bade fair to become a perdition as bad as any that Brother Sodom ever depicted. And against these on the one side, and the Brother Sodoms on the other, I shall interrupt my story to put this chapter under shelter of that wise remark of the great Dr. Adam Clarke, who says, "The fear of God is the beginning of wisdom, the terror of God confounds the soul"; and that other saying of his: "With the *fear* of God the love of God is ever consistent; but where the *terror* of the Lord reigns, there can neither be *fear, faith,* nor *love;* nay, nor *hope* either." And yet I am not sure that even the Brother Sodoms were made in vain.

On this evening Mr. Soden was as terrible as usual. Bud heard him without flinching. Small, who sat farther forward, listened with pious approval. Mr. Soden, out of distorted figures pieced together from different passages of Scripture, built a hell, not quite Miltonic, nor yet Dantean, but as Miltonic and Dantean as his unrefined imagination could make it. As he rose toward his climax of hideous description, Walter Johnson trembled from head to foot and sat close to Bud. Then, as burly Mr. Soden, with great gusto, depicted materialistic tortures that startled the nerves of everybody except Bud, Walter

153

wanted to leave, but Bud would not let him. For some
reason he wished to keep his companion in the crucible
as long as possible.

"Young man!" cried Mr. Soden, and the explosive voice
seemed to come from the hell that he had created—
"young man! you who have followed the counsel of evil
companions"—here he paused and looked about, as if
trying to find the man he wanted, while Walter crept
up close to Bud and shaded his face—"I mean you who
have chosen evil pursuits, and who can not get free from
bad habits and associations that are dragging you down
to hell! You are standing on the very crumbling brink
of hell to-night. The smell of the brimstone is on your
garments; the hot breath of hell is in your face! The devils
are waiting for you! Delay and you are damned! You
may die before daylight! You may never get out that
door! The awful angel of death is just ready to strike you
down!" Here some shrieked with terror, others sobbed,
and Brother Sodom looked with approval on the storm he
had awakened. The very harshness of his tone, his lofty
egotism of manner, that which had roused all Bud's combativeness, shook poor Walter as a wind would shake a
reed. In the midst of the general excitement he seized
his hat and hastened out the door. Bud followed, while
Soden shot his lightnings after them, declaring that
"young men who ran away from the truth would dwell in
torments forever."

Bud had not counted amiss when he thought that Mr.
Soden's preaching would be likely to arouse so mean
spirited a fellow as Walter. So vivid was the impression
that Johnson begged Bud to return to the office with him.
He felt sick, and was afraid that he should die before
morning. He insisted that Bud should stay with him all

night. To this Means readily consented, and by morning he had heard all that the frightened Walter had to tell.

And now let us return to the trial, where Ralph sits waiting the testimony of Walter Johnson, which is to prove his statement false.

XXXI

The Trial Concluded

I do not know how much interest the "gentle reader" may feel in Bud. With me, he is a favorite. And I venture to hope that there are some Buddhists among my readers who will wish the contradictoriness of his actions explained. The first dash of disappointment had well-nigh upset him. And when a man concludes to throw overboard his good resolutions, he always seeks to avoid the witness of those resolutions. Hence Bud, after that distressful Tuesday evening on which Miss Martha had given him "the sack," wished to see Ralph less than any one else. And yet when he came to suspect Small's villainy, his whole nature revolted at it. But having broken with Ralph, he thought it best to maintain an attitude of apparent hostility, that he might act as a detective, and perhaps, save his friend from the mischief that threatened him. As soon as he heard of Ralph's arrest, he determined to make Walter Johnson tell his own secret in court, because he knew that it would be best for Ralph that Walter should tell it. Bud's telling at second hand would not be conclusive. And he sincerely desired to save Walter from prison. For Walter Johnson was the victim of Dr. Small, or of Dr. Small and such novels as "The Pirate's Bride," "Claude Duval," "The Wild Rover of the West Indies," and the cheap biographies of such men as Murrell. Small found him with his imagination

flamed by the history of such heroes, and opened to
im the path to glory for which he longed.

The whole morning after Ralph's arrest, Bud was work-
g on Walter's conscience and his fears. The poor fellow,
nable to act for himself, was torn asunder between the
ld ascendency of Small and the new ascendency of Bud
Means. Bud finally frightened him, by the fear of the
enitentiary, into going to the place of trial. But once
side the door, and once in sight of Small, who was more
 him than God, or, rather, more to him than the devil—
r the devil was Walter's God, or, perhaps, I should say,
Valter's God was a devil—once in sight of Small, he
fused to move an inch farther. And Bud, after all his
erseverance, was about to give up in sheer despair.

Fortunately, just at that moment Small's desire to re-
eve himself from the taint of suspicion and to crush
alph as completely as possible, made him overshoot the
ark by asking that Walter be called to the stand, as we
ave before recounted. He knew that he had no tool so
pple as the cowardly Walter. In the very language of
e request, he had given Walter an intimation of what he
anted him to swear to. Walter listened to Small's words
 to his doom. He felt that he should die of indecision.
he perdition of a man of his stamp is to have to make
p his mind. Such men generally fall back on some one
ore positive, and take all their resolutions ready-made.
ut here Walter must decide for himself. For the con-
able was already calling his name; the court, the spec-
tors, and, most of all, Dr. Small, were waiting for him.
e moved forward mechanically through the dense
owd, Bud following part of the way to whisper, "Tell
e truth or go to penitentiary." Walter shook and shiv-
red at this. The witness with difficulty held up his hand
ng enough to be sworn.

157

"Please tell the court," said Bronson, "whether you know anything of the whereabouts of Dr. Small on the night of the robbery at Peter Schroeder's."

Small had detected Walter's agitation, and, taking alarm, had edged his way around so as to stand full in Walter's sight, and there, with keen, magnetic eye on the weak orbs of the young man, he was able to assume his old position, and sway the fellow absolutely.

"On the night of the robbery"—Walter's voice was weak, but he seemed to be reading his answer out of Small's eyes—"on the night of the robbery Dr. Small came home before——" here the witness stopped and shook and shivered again. For Bud, detecting the effect of Small's gaze, had pushed his great hulk in front of Small, and had fastened his eyes on Walter with a look that said, "Tell the truth or go to penitentiary."

"I can't, I can't. O God! what shall I do?" the witness exclaimed, answering the look of Bud. For it seemed to him that Bud had spoken. To the people and the court this agitation was inexplicable. Squire Hawkins's wig got awry, his glass eye turned in toward his nose, and he had great difficulty in keeping his teeth from falling out. The excitement became painfully intense. Ralph was on his feet, looking at the witness, and feeling that somehow Bud and Dr. Small—his good angel and his demon—were playing an awful game, of which he was the stake. The crowd swayed to and fro, but remained utterly silent, waiting to hear the least whisper from the witness, who stood trembling a moment with his hands over his face, and then fainted.

The fainting of a person in a crowd is a signal for everybody else to make fools of themselves. There was a rush toward the fainting man, there was a cry for water. Everybody asked everybody else to open the windows

158

and everybody wished everybody else to stand back and give him air. But nobody opened the window, and nobody stood back. The only perfectly cool man in the room was Small. With a quiet air of professional authority he pushed forward and felt the patient's pulse, remarking to the court that he thought it was a sudden attack of fever with delirium. When Walter revived, Dr. Small would have removed him, but Ralph insisted that his testimony should be heard. Under pretense of watching his patient, Small kept close to him. And Walter began the same old story about Dr. Small's having arrived at the office before eleven o'clock, when Bud came up behind the doctor and fastened his eyes on the witness with the same significant look, and Walter, with visions of the penitentiary before him, halted, stammered, and seemed about to faint again.

"If the court please," said Bronson, "this witness is evidently intimidated by that stout young man," pointing to Bud. "I have seen him twice interrupt witness's testimony by casting threatening looks at him. I trust the court will have him removed from the court-room."

After a few moments' consultation, during which Squire Hawkins held his wig in place with one hand and alternately adjusted his eye and his spectacles with the other, the magistrates, who were utterly bewildered by the turn things were taking, decided that it could do no harm, and that it was best to try the experiment of removing Bud. Perhaps Johnson would then be able to get through with his testimony. The constable therefor asked Bud if he would please leave the room. Bud cast one last look at the witness and walked out like a captive bear.

Ralph stood watching the receding form of Bud. The emergency had made him as cool as Small ever was. Bud stopped at the door, where he was completely out of sight of the witness, concealed by the excited spectators, who stood on the benches to see what was going on in front.

"The witness will please proceed," said Bronson.

"If the court please"—it was Ralph who spoke—"I believe I have as much at stake in this trial as any one. That witness is evidently intimidated. But not by Mr. Means. I ask that Dr. Small be removed out of sight of the witness."

"A most extraordinary request, truly." This was what Small's bland countenance said; he did not open his lips.

"It's no more than fair," said Squire Hawkins, adjusting his wig, "that the witness be relieved of everything that anybody might think affects his voracity in this matter."

Dr. Small, giving Walter one friendly, appealing look, moved back by the door, and stood alongside Bud, as meek, quiet, and disinterested as any man in the house.

"The witness will now proceed with his testimony." This time it was Squire Hawkins who spoke. Bronson had been attacked with a suspicion that this witness was not just what he wanted, and had relapsed into silence.

Walter's struggle was by no means ended by the disappearance of Small and Bud. There came the recollection of his mother's stern face—a face which had never been a motive toward the right, but only a goad to deception. What would she say if he should confess? Just as he had recovered himself, and was about to repeat the old lie which had twice died upon his lips at the sight of Bud's look, he caught sight of another face, which made him tremble again. It was the lofty and terrible countenance of Mr. Soden. One might have thought, from the expression it wore, that the seven last vials were in his hands,

160

the seven apocalyptic trumpets waiting for his lips, and the seven thunders sitting upon his eyebrows. The moment that Walter saw him he smelled the brimstone on his own garments, he felt himself upon the crumbling brink of the precipice, with perdition below him. Now I am sure that "Brother Sodoms" were not made wholly in vain. There are plenty of mean-spirited men like Walter Johnson, whose feeble consciences need all the support they can get from the fear of perdition, and who are incapable of any other conception of it than a coarse and materialistic one. Let us set it down to the credit of Brother Sodom, with his stiff stock, his thunderous face, and his awful walk, that his influence over Walter was on the side of truth.

"Please proceed," said Squire Hawkins to Walter. The Squire's wig lay on one side, he had forgotten to adjust his eye, and he leaned forward, tremulous with interest.

"Well, then," said Walter, looking not at the court nor at Bronson nor at the prisoner, but furtively at Mr. Soden—"well, then, if I must"—and Mr. Soden's awful face seemed to answer that he surely must—"well, then, I hope you won't send me to prison"—this to Squire Hawkins, whose face re-assured him—"but—oh! I don't see how I can!" But one look at Mr. Soden assured him that he could and that he must, and so, with an agony painful to the spectators, he told the story in driblets. How, while yet in Lewisburg, he had been made a member of a gang of which Small was chief; how they concealed from him the names of all the band except six, of whom the Joneses and Small were three.

Here and there was a scuffle at the door. The court demanded silence.

"Dr. Small's trying to git out, plague take him," said

Bud, who stood with his back planted against the door. "I'd like the court to send and git his trunk afore he has a chance to burn up all the papers that's in it."

"Constable, you will arrest Dr. Small, Peter Jones, and William Jones. Send two deputies to bring Small's trunk into court," said Squire Underwood.

The prosecuting attorney was silent.

Walter then told of the robbery at Schroeder's, told where he and Small had whittled the fence while the Joneses entered the house, and confirmed Ralph's story by telling how they had seen Ralph in a fence-corner, and how they had met the basket-maker on the hill.

"*To* be sure," said the old man, who had not ventured to hold up his head, after he was arrested, until Walter began his testimony.

Walter felt inclined to stop, but he could not do it, for there stood Mr. Soden, looking to him like a messenger from the skies, or the bottomless pit, sent to extort the last word from his guilty soul. He felt that he was making a clean breast of it at the risk of perdition, with the penitentiary thrown in, if he faltered. And so he told the whole thing as though it had been the day of doom, and by the time he was through, Small's trunk was in court.

Here a new hubbub took place at the door. It was none other than the crazy pauper, Tom Bifield, who personated General Andrew Jackson in the poor-house. He had caught some inkling of the trial, and had escaped in Bill Jones's absence. His red plume was flying, and in his tattered and filthy garb he was indeed a picturesque figure.

"Squar," said he, elbowing his way through the crowd, "I kin tell you somethin'. I'm Gineral Andrew Jackson. Lost my head at Bueny Visty. This head growed on. It

'n't good fer much. One side's tater. But t'other's sound
s a nut. Now, I kin give you information."

Bronson, with the quick perceptions of a politician,
ıad begun to see which way future winds would prob-
ıbly blow. "If the court please," he said, "this man is
ıot wholly sane, but we might get valuable information
ɔut of him. I suggest that his testimony be taken for
vhat it is worth."

"No, you don't swar me," broke in the lunatic. "Not if
I know's myself. You see, when a feller's got one side of
his head tater, he's mighty onsartain like. You don't swar
me, fer I can't tell what minute the tater side'll begin to
talk. I'm talkin' out of the lef' side now, and I'm all right.
But you don't swar me. But ef you'll send some of your
constables out to the barn at the pore-house and look
under the hay-mow in the north-east corner, you'll find
some things may be as has been a missin' fer some time.
And that a'n't out of the tater side nuther."

Meantime Bud did not rest. Hearing the nature of the
testimony given by Hank Banta before he entered, he
attacked Hank and vowed he'd send him to prison if he
didn't make a clean breast. Hank was a thorough coward,
and, now that his friends were prisoners, was ready
enough to tell the truth if he could be protected from
prosecution. Seeing the disposition of the prosecuting attorney, Bud got from him a promise that he would do
what he could to protect Hank. That worthy then took
the stand, confessed his lie, and even told the inducement
which Mr. Pete Jones had offered him to perjure himself.

"*To* be sure," said Pearson.

Squire Hawkins, turning his right eye upon him, while
the left looked at the ceiling, said: "Be careful, Mr. Pearson, or I shall have to punish you for contempt."

163

"Why, Squar, I didn't know 'twas any sin to hev a healthy contemp' fer sech a thief as Jones!"

The Squire looked at Mr. Pearson severely, and the latter, feeling that he had committed some offense without knowing it, subsided into silence.

Bronson now had a keen sense of the direction of the gale.

"If the court please," said he, "I have tried to do my duty in this case. It was my duty to prosecute Mr. Hartsook, however much I might feel assured that he was innocent, and that he would be able to prove his innocence. I now enter a *nolle* in his case and that of John Pearson, and I ask that this court adjourn until to-morrow, in order to give me time to examine the evidence in the case of the other parties under arrest. I am proud to think that my efforts have been the means of sifting the matter to the bottom, of freeing Mr. Hartsook from suspicion, and of detecting the real criminals."

"Ugh!" said Mr. Pearson, who conceived a great dislike to Bronson.

"The court," said Squire Hawkins, "congratulates Mr. Hartsook on his triumphant acquittal. He is discharged from the bar of this court, and from the bar of public sentiment, without a suspicion of guilt. Constable, discharge Ralph Hartsook and John Pearson."

Old Jack Means, who had always had a warm side for the master, now proposed three cheers for Mr. Hartsook and they were given with a will by the people who would have hanged him an hour before.

Mrs. Means gave it as her opinion that "Jack Means allers wuz a fool!"

"This court," said Dr. Underwood, "has one other duty to perform before adjourning for the day. Recall Hannah Thomson."

164

"I jist started her on ahead to git supper and milk the ows," said Mrs. Means. "A'n't agoin' to have her loafin' ere all day."

"Constable, recall her. This court can not adjourn until he returns!"

Hannah had gone but a little way, and was soon in the resence of the court, trembling for fear of some new alamity.

"Hannah Thomson"—it was Squire Underwood who poke—"Hannah Thomson, this court wishes to ask you ne or two questions."

"Yes, sir," but her voice died to a whisper.

"How old did you say you were?"

"Eighteen, sir, last October."

"Can you prove your age?"

"Yes, sir—by my mother."

"For how long are you bound to Mr. Means?"

"Till I'm twenty-one."

"This court feels in duty bound to inform you that, ccording to the laws of Indiana, a woman is of age at ighteen, and as no indenture could be made binding fter you had reached your majority, you are the victim f a deception. You are free, and if it can be proven that ou have been defrauded by a willful deception, a suit or damages will lie."

"Ugh!" said Mrs. Means. "You're a purty court, a'n't ou, Dr. Underwood?"

"Be careful, Mrs. Means, or I shall have to fine you for ontempt of court."

But the people, who were in the cheering humor, heered Hannah and the justices, and then cheered Ralph gain. Granny Sanders shook hands with him, and allers nowed he'd come out right. It allers 'peared like as if)r. Small warn't jist the sort to tie to, you know. And old John Pearson went home, after drinking two or three glasses of Welch's whisky, keeping time to an imaginary triumphal march, and feeling prouder than he had ever felt since he fit the Britishers under Scott at Lundy's Lane. He told his wife that the master had jist knocked the hind-sights offen that air young lawyer from Lewisburg.

Walter was held to bail that he might appear as a witness, and Ralph might have sent his aunt a Roland for an Oliver. But he only sent a note to his uncle, asking him to go Walter's bail. If he had been resentful, he could not have wished for a more complete revenge than the day had brought.

XXXII

After the Battle

Nothing can be more demoralizing in the long run than lynch law. And yet lynch law often originates in a burst of generous indignation which is not willing to suffer a bold oppressor to escape by means of corrupt and cowardly courts. It is oftener born of fear. Both motives powerfully agitated the people of the region round about Clifty as night drew on after Ralph's acquittal. They were justly indignant that Ralph had been made the victim of such a conspiracy, and they were frightened at the unseen danger to the community from such a band as that of Small's. It was certain that they did not know the full extent of the danger as yet. And what Small might do with a jury, or what Pete Jones might do with a sheriff, was a question. I must not detain the reader to tell how the mob rose. Nobody knows how such things come about. Their origin is as inexplicable as that of an earthquake. But, at any rate, a rope was twice put round Small's neck during that night, and both times Small was saved only by the nerve and address of Ralph, who had learned how unjust mob law may be. As for Small, he neither trembled when they were ready to hang him, nor looked relieved when he was saved, nor showed the slightest flush of penitence or gratitude. He bore himself in a quiet, gentlemanly way throughout, like the admirable villain that he was.

He waived a preliminary examination the next day; his

father went his bail, and he forfeited his bail and disappeared from the county and from the horizon of my story. Two reports concerning Small have been in circulation—one that he was running a faro-bank in San Francisco, the other that he was curing consumption by inhalation and electricity here in New York. If this latter were true, it would leave it an open question whether Ralph did well to save him from the gallows. Pete Jones and Bill, as usually happens to the rougher villains, went to prison, and when their terms had expired moved to Pike County, Missouri.

But it is about Hannah that you want to hear, and that I want to tell. She went straight from the court-room to Flat Creek, climbed to her chamber, packed all her earthly goods, consisting chiefly of a few family relics, in a handkerchief, and turned her back on the house of Means forever. At the gate she met the old woman, who shook her fist in the girl's face and gave her a parting benediction in the words: "You mis'able, ongrateful critter you, go 'long! I'm glad to be shed of you!" At the barn she met Bud, and he told her good-by with a little huskiness in his voice, while a tear glistened in her eye. Bud had been a friend in need, and such a friend one does not leave without a pang.

"Where are you going? Can I——"

"No, no!" And with that she hastened on, afraid that Bud would offer to hitch up the roan colt. And she did not want to add to his domestic unhappiness by compromising him in that way.

It was dusk and raining when she left. The hours were long, the road was lonely, and after the revelations of that day it did not seem wholly safe. But from the moment that she found herself free, her heart had been ready to break with an impatient home-sickness. What though there might be robbers in the woods? What though there were ten rough miles to travel? What though the rain was in her face? What though she had not tasted food since the morning of that exciting day? Flat Creek and bondage were behind; freedom, mother, Shocky, and home were before her, and her feet grew lighter with the thought. And if she needed any other joy, it was to know that the master was clear. And he would come! And so she traversed the weary distance, and so she inquired and found the house, the beautiful, homely old house of beautiful, homely old Nancy Sawyer, and knocked, and was admitted, and fell down, faint and weary, at her blind mother's feet, and laid her tired head in her mother's lap and wept, and wept like a child, and said, "O mother! I'm free, I'm free!" while the mother's tears baptized her face, and the mother's trembling fingers combed out her tresses. And Shocky stood by her and cried: "I knowed God wouldn't forget you, Hanner!"

Hannah was ready now to do anything by which she could support her mother and Shocky. She was strong, and inured to toil. She was willing and cheerful, and she would gladly have gone to service if by that means she could have supported the family. And, for that matter, her mother was already nearly able to support herself by her knitting. But Hannah had been carefully educated when young, and at that moment the old public schools were being organized into a graded school, and the good minister, who shall be nameless, because he is, perhaps, still living in Indiana, and who in Methodist parlance was called "the preacher-in-charge of Lewisburg Station" —this good minister and Miss Nancy Sawyer got Hannah a place as teacher of a primary department. And then a little house with four rooms was rented, and a little, a very little furniture was put into it, and the old, sweet home was established again. The father was gone, never to come back again. But the rest were here. And somehow Hannah kept waiting for somebody else to come.

XXXIII

Into the Light

For two weeks longer Ralph taught at the Flat Creek school-house. He was everybody's hero. And he was Bud's idol. He did what he could to get Bud and Martha together, and though Bud always "saw her safe home" after this, and called on her every Sunday evening, yet, to save his life, he could not forget his big fists and his big feet long enough to say what he most wanted to say, and what Martha most wanted him to say.

At the end of two weeks Ralph found himself exceedingly weary of Flat Creek, and exceedingly glad to hear from Mr. Means that the school-money had "gin aout." It gave him a good excuse to return to Lewisburg, where his heart and his treasure were. A certain sense of delicacy had kept him from writing to Hannah just yet.

When he got to Lewisburg he had good news. His uncle, ashamed of his previous neglect, and perhaps with an eye to his nephew's growing popularity, had gotten him the charge of the grammar department in the new graded school in the village. So he quietly arranged to board at a boarding-house. His aunt could not have him about, of which fact he was very glad. She could not but feel, she said, that he might have taken better care of Walter than he did, when they were only four miles apart.

He did not hasten to call on Hannah. Why should he? He sent her a message, of no consequence in itself, by

Nancy Sawyer. Then he took possession of his school; and then, on the evening of the first day of school, he went, as he had appointed to himself, to see Hannah Thomson.

And she, with some sweet presentiment, had gotten things ready by fixing up the scantily-furnished room as well as she could. And Miss Nancy Sawyer, who had seen Ralph that afternoon, had guessed that he was going to see Hannah. It's wonderful how much enjoyment a generous heart can get out of the happiness of others. Is not that what He meant when he said of such as Miss Sawyer that they should have a hundred-fold in this life for all their sacrifices? Did not Miss Nancy enjoy a hundred weddings, and love and have the love of five hundred children? And so Miss Nancy just happened over at Mrs. Thomson's humble home, and, just in the most matter-of-course way, asked that lady and Shocky to come over to her house. Shocky wanted Hannah to come too. But Hannah blushed a little, and said that she would rather not.

And when she was left alone, Hannah fixed her hair two or three times, and swept the hearth, and moved the chairs first one way and then another, and did a good many other needless things. Needless: for a lover, if he be lover, does not see furniture or dress.

And then she sat down by the fire, and tried to sew, and tried to look unconcerned, and tried to feel unconcerned, and tried not to expect anybody, and tried to make her heart keep still. And tried in vain. For a gentle rap at the door sent her pulse up twenty beats a minute and made her face burn. And Hartsook was, for the first time, abashed in the presence of Hannah. For the oppressed girl had, in two weeks, blossomed out into the full-blown woman.

And Ralph sat down by the fire, and talked of his

172

school and her school, and everything else but what he wanted to talk about. And then the conversation drifted back to Flat Creek, and to the walk through the pasture, and to the box-alder tree, and to the painful talk in the lane. And Hannah begged to be forgiven, and Ralph laughed at the idea that she had done anything wrong. And she praised his goodness to Shocky, and he drew her little note out of—— But I agreed not to tell you where he kept it. And then she blushed, and he told how the note had sustained him, and how her white face kept up his courage in his flight down the bed of Clifty Creek. And he sat a little nearer, to show her the note that he had carried in his bosom—— I have told it! And——but I must not proceed. A love-scene, ever so beautiful in itself, will not bear telling. And so I shall leave a little gap just here, which you may fill up as you please. . . . . Somehow, they never knew how, they got to talking about the future instead of the past, after that, and to planning their two lives as one life. And . . . . And when Miss Nancy and Mrs. Thomson returned later in the evening, Ralph was standing by the mantel-piece, but Shocky noticed that his chair was close to Hannah's. And good Miss Nancy Sawyer looked in Hannah's face and was happy.

XXXIV

"How It Came Out"

We are all children in reading stories. We want more tha
all else to know how it all came out at the end, and, i
our taste is not perverted, we like it to come out wel
For my part, ever since I began to write this story,
have been anxious to know how it was going to come ou

Well, there were very few invited. It took place at te
in the morning. The "preacher-in-charge" came, of cours
Miss Nancy Sawyer was there. But Ralph's uncle wa
away, and Aunt Matilda had a sore throat and couldn
come. Perhaps the memory of the fact that she ha
refused Mrs. Thomson, the pauper, a bed for two night
affected her throat. But Miss Nancy and her sister wer
there, and the preacher. And that was all, beside th
family, and Bud and Martha. Of course Bud and Marth
came. And driving Martha to a wedding in a "jumpe
was the one opportunity Bud needed. His hands wer
busy, his big boots were out of sight, and it was so eas
to slip from Ralph's love affair to his own, that Bud som
how, in pulling Martha Hawkins's shawl about her, stam
mered out half a proposal, which Martha, generous sou
took for the whole ceremony, and accepted. And Bud wa
so happy that Ralph guessed from his face and voice tha
the agony was over, and Bud was betrothed at last to th
"gal as was a gal."

And after Ralph and Hannah were married—there wa
no trip, Ralph only changed his boarding-place and b

174

came head of the house at Mrs. Thomson's thereafter—after it was all over, Bud came to Mr. Hartsook, and, snickering just a little, said as how as him and Martha had fixed it all up, and now they wanted to ax his advice; and Martha, proud but blushing, came up and nodded assent. Bud said as how as he hadn't got no book-larnin' nor nothin', and as how as he wanted to be somethin', and put in his best licks fer Him, you know. And that Marthy, she was of the same way of thinkin', and that was a blessin'. And the Squire was a goin' to marry agin', and Marthy would ruther vacate. And his mother and Mirandy was sech as he wouldn't take no wife to. And he thought as how Mr. Hartsook might think of some way or some place where he and Marthy mout make a livin' fer the present, and put in their best licks fer Him, you know.

Ralph thought a moment. He was about to make an allusion to Hercules and the Augean stables, but he remembered that Bud would not understand it, though it might remind Martha of something she had seen at the East, the time she was to Bosting.

"Bud, my dear friend," said Ralph, "it looks a little hard to ask you to take a new wife"—here Bud looked admiringly at Martha—"to the poor-house. But I don't know anywhere where you can do so much good for Christ as by taking charge of that place, and I can get the appointment for you. The new commissioners want just such a man."

"What d'ye say, Marthy?" said Bud.

"Why, somebody ought to do for the poor, and I should like to do it."

And so Hercules cleaned the Augean stables.

And so my humble, homely Hoosier story of twenty years ago draws to a close, and, not without regret, I take leave of Ralph, and Hannah, and Shocky, and Bud, and Martha, and Miss Nancy, and of my readers.

P. S.—A copy of the Lewisburg *Jeffersonian* came into my hands to-day, and I see by its columns that Ralph Hartsook is principal of the Lewisburg Academy. It took me some time, however, to make out that the sheriff of the county, Mr. Israel W. Means, was none other than my old friend Bud, of the Church of the Best Licks. I was almost as much puzzled over his name as I was when I saw an article in a city paper, by Prof. W. J. Thomson, on Poor-Houses. I should not have recognized the writer as Shocky, had I not known that Shocky has given all his spare time to making outcasts feel that God has not forgot. For, indeed, God never forgets. But some of those to whom he intrusts his work do forget.

AMERICAN CENTURY SERIES

WHEN ORDERING, please use the Standard Book Number consisting of the publisher's prefix, 8090–, plus the five digits following each title. (Note that the numbers given in this list are for paperback editions only. Many of the books are also available in cloth.)